Father's Big Improvements

By CAROLINE D. EMERSON

Illustrated by E. R. Kinstler

SCHOLASTIC BOOK SERVICES

Published by Scholastic Book Services, a division of Scholastic Magazines, Inc., 33 West 42nd Street, New York 36, N. Y.

Printing History

1st printing......................August, 1960
2nd printing......................October, 1960

Printed in the U.S.A.

CONTENTS

A Foreword on Faucets and Furnaces

Water runs in pipes!

Switches snap lights on and off!

Wires carry messages all over town!

Why, of course they do! What nonsense not to know that!

Well, they didn't *always*, you know. In every old house there was a "first time" when the faucets were turned and the running water ran. There was a "first time" when the fire was lighted in the new furnace. To children growing up in the 1880's and 1890's it was all very exciting.

Big cities and big towns had "improvements" first. In no two places did they come in just the same order, and some small villages don't have them yet. These stories will tell you of what happened in one house in one small town in New England. If you read it you will learn all about

FATHER'S

BIG

IMPROVEMENTS.

1. The Marshall Family

When Jimmie Marshall was four years old he wore white shirts with wide ruffled collars and a kilted skirt. His hair hung down his back in long curls.

He had to dress that way! His mother made him!

But in the year 1888 many little boys wore long curls and ruffled shirts and kilted skirts, so Jimmy did not mind them much.

His sister, Nan Marshall, had just been born. When Jimmie heard that he had a new baby sister he went to Mr. Jones who lived next door to the Marshall house. Mr. Jones had a litter of collie pups. Jimmie suggested trading one puppy for the new baby.

"Oh, no!" said Mr. Jones. "I shouldn't know what to do with such a small baby. But perhaps you'll need a puppy to help take care of her."

Jimmie knelt eagerly beside the pile of wiggling, yellow fur balls. From one ball a wet nose poked up into his face and a tongue licked his cheek.

"I'd like this one," said Jimmie and he gathered the puppy into his arms.

So Nan and Bouncer, the collie pup, came into the Marshall family on the same day, and a very bad day it was, for Nan was born just at the beginning of The Great Blizzard of 1888.

People still talk of the Great Blizzard of 1888 and well they may! Never before in the memory of man had there been such a snowstorm and never has there been such a storm since. The snow fell all the afternoon. The snow fell all night long. The snow piled up to the porch railing. The snow piled up to the kitchen window. The snow piled up until—but that comes later in the story.

Mrs. Jones kept Jimmie and Bouncer at her house, and there the boy and the puppy stood at the window and watched the snow come down. But back at the Marshall house no one had time to look out of the window. Everybody was far too busy with the new baby. For Nan cried and cried and would not stop. Mrs. Marshall was very ill indeed, and Mr. Marshall and Grandmother were much worried.

As the doctor left the house he shook his head.

"I wish you could get that nurse who lives in the last house at the foot of the hill," he said. "She's a good nurse and a clever nurse and she might know what to do for that baby."

"Very well," said Mr. Marshall firmly. "I'll get that nurse."

So Mr. Marshall went to the telephone—

Oh, no, he didn't!

There were no telephones in country towns in 1888, so Mr. Marshall did not call up the nurse on the telephone to ask her to come to take care of Nan. He had never seen a telephone.

So Mr. Marshall went out to the garage and took out the car—

Oh, no, he didn't!

There were no automobiles in those days except a few

strange-looking things that inventors were working on. So Mr. Marshall put on his hat and overcoat and took the street car at the corner—

Oh, no, he didn't!

There were no street cars and no buses in country towns in the year 1888.

The Marshalls didn't even keep a horse. They lived close to the village. Mr. Marshall walked to his office, and Mrs. Marshall walked to the stores.

Walking was just what Mr. Marshall had to do now. He put on his heavy top coat and pulled a cap down round his ears.

"Gracious me!" said Grandmother as she looked out the window. "I never saw such a storm."

Mr. Marshall pulled on high rubber boots.

"You'd better take an extra pair for the nurse to wear," said Grandmother, "if she's to get here tonight in this snow."

So Mr. Marshall found an extra pair of boots. He put one under his right arm and one under his left arm. Then he opened the door.

He was greeted with a gust of wind and a cloud of snow. Quickly he closed the door behind him and stepped out into the storm.

2. The Great Blizzard

As Mr. Marshall stepped off the porch he sank into snow up to his knees. There was no path and there were no tracks except those left by the doctor, and they were nearly filled by now with more soft heavy snow. Mr. Marshall waded out to the road. He could tell where the road was only by the trees on either side. For there was no break in the thick, white blanket that covered everything. The air was so full of the soft, fluffy flakes that it was hard to see.

Mr. Marshall stopped for a moment to be sure of his directions. It was only three in the afternoon, but already dim lights came from neighbors' lamps. Stores and offices were closed and everyone had hurried home to safety as the storm began. Mr. Marshall wiped the snow from his face and started on again.

"There's no time to waste," he thought. "If the storm keeps on like this there will be no getting home again in a couple of hours."

Then he thought of the baby and how she cried. Snow or no snow, he would get that nurse.

Down Prospect Hill went Mr. Marshall.

"It is easier getting down this hill than it will be getting up again," he thought grimly, but he wasn't turning back.

At the bottom of the hill he groped his way through the snow to the door of a little white house. A light shone dimly from the kitchen window. Mr. Marshall beat on the door with his fist.

The door opened one inch.

"Who is there?" asked a very firm voice.

"I'm Mr. Marshall and I need a nurse," he called.

"What is the matter with you?" asked the same very firm voice.

"There is nothing the matter with me," explained Mr. Marshall. "It's my very small daughter at home. She's a new tiny baby and she does nothing but cry. She needs you to look after her."

At the mention of a baby the nurse opened the door quickly to let in as little wind and snow as possible. She pulled Mr. Marshall hurriedly inside. When she saw how white and tired he was she pushed him over to a chair by the cracking fire. Then she hurried to get a cup of coffee from the pot on the stove. She did not ask any more questions until he had drunk the coffee and lay back resting in the kitchen rocker. His clothes began to steam from the heat. He pulled off his gloves and began to rub his hands.

"Do you expect me to go out on a night like this?" asked the nurse.

"Well," said Mr. Marshall thoughtfully, "she's the very smallest baby you ever saw, and she does nothing but cry."

"I have seen small babies in my day," said the nurse.

"None so small as this one!" said Mr. Marshall.

"Well—" replied the nurse, "how do you expect me to get there?"

"I brought these for you to wear," said Mr. Marshall as he laid the extra rubber boots on the floor. "You can walk behind me and step in my footsteps."

The nurse looked at the rubber boots and she looked at Mr. Marshall. He was very much afraid that she was going to tell him to take his boots and go home. Instead she went to the closet and took down a heavy coat, a knitted cap, and a muffler. She put them on and then pulled on the rubber boots. Mr. Marshall gave a sigh of relief. They both drank cups of black coffee, and the nurse shut up the stove and put out the fire in the fireplace.

Then she said firmly, "Hurry up!" just as though it had been Mr. Marshall who had kept her waiting. Mr. Marshall jumped to his feet and pulled on his gloves.

Carefully they stepped out into the strange, white world. Stumbling, they struggled through the mass of snow.

"Look out!" cried Mr. Marshall as his foot sank down into the ditch. "The road must be over here."

The nurse's mouth was buried in her muffler.

"Keep to the right of that tree," she mumbled.

Mr. Marshall tripped over a stone and fell into a snow bank. He felt a firm hand jerk him to his feet. Then he struggled to get his balance again.

"There you are," said the nurse, "and here's the road. If we keep going straight for the hill there ought not to be any more ditches to fall into or stone walls to stumble over. Keep going!"

On and on went Mr. Marshall. It seemed as if he lifted a ton of snow with every step. Twice he got off the road. Twice he stumbled into the ditch. After that he sat in the snow and rested for a few seconds before he had strength to go on. When the nurse thought he had rested long enough she jerked him to his feet. And well it was that she did! Many a person sat down to rest in that storm who never had strength to rise again.

At last they reached the top of the hill. Once they stopped at a farmhouse for hot coffee and a minute's warmth, but they did not dare stop long.

"Good luck to you," cried the farmer and his wife as they held the lamp at the door. But its light shone only a few yards down the path, so dense was the cloud of snow.

At last Mr. Marshall saw the dim shape of his own house just ahead. A faint light twinkled from the kitchen window.

"Here we are!" shouted Mr. Marshall.

"And a good thing we are," muttered the nurse. "I wouldn't go another step, not if you had twins!"

At the sound of their voices Grandmother threw open the door.

"Thank goodness you are here and safe!" she cried.

In another minute they were inside. Grandmother was pulling off their coats and rubbing their poor nipped hands and pouring hot coffee. Mr. Marshall sat by the stove and closed his eyes. He was so tired that he could scarcely keep awake.

But as soon as the nurse was warm she put on her apron.

"Let me see that baby," she said.

3. Snow and More Snow

No one slept much in the Marshall house that night. Nan kept crying and moaning. The nurse heated logs of wood and packed them around the tiny mite to keep her warm. She even slipped the baby's basket into the oven and sat beside the open door to be sure that it did not grow too warm inside. She fed Nan with drops of warmed milk. Then towards midnight Nan fell asleep and the Marshall family gave a sigh of relief.

"I'll pull that baby through yet," said the nurse.

Mr. Marshall was busy all night keeping the fires going and bringing in coal and wood from the woodshed. It was hard to keep the house warm enough for the new baby. The wind was beating against the windows and rattling the blinds.

It was so cold that Mr. Marshall went down the cellar to open the drafts on the furnace.

Oh, no, he didn't!

There was no furnace in the Marshall house in the year 1888 when Nan was born. There was the big cooking stove in the kitchen and another coal stove in the dining room. There were little iron gratings in the floor above the stoves to let heat through to the bedrooms above, but bedrooms were cold places in 1888.

When Mr. Marshall wanted to warm the house, he

carried in coal and built up the fires in the kitchen stove and the dining-room stove. Grandmother could remember the days before coal when all the fires were kept going with logs of wood!

Mr. Marshall lifted the tea-kettle on the stove to see if there was hot water. It was nearly empty and he went to the sink to fill it. He turned the faucet—

Oh, no, he didn't!

There was no running water in the Marshall house in those days. Mr. Marshall filled the kettle from the pump which stood by the kitchen sink. All the water that the Marshalls used came from the pump. Way down under the house was a deep well of cold, clear water. The pump pulled up the water when the Marshalls needed it.

The room seemed rather dark, so Mr. Marshall put out his hand to turn on another electric light—

Oh, no, he didn't!

There were no electric lights in the Marshall house in those days. Mr. Marshall turned up the wick of the kerosene lamp and sat down to read his paper for a few minutes.

"This night certainly seems long," said the nurse. "What time is it anyway?"

"Yes," said Grandmother, "it doesn't seem as if morning would ever come."

Mr. Marshall took out his watch. He looked at it. He put it to his ear. He gave it a little shake.

"Why, it can't be!" said Mr. Marshall in amazement.

"Can't be what?" asked the nurse firmly.

"My watch says eight o'clock," said Mr. Marshall and he got up and went in to look at the dining-room clock.

"Why, it is as dark as night!" cried Grandmother.

"Is it eight o'clock last night or tomorrow morning?" asked Mr. Marshall.

"What has happened?" cried Grandmother.

They all ran to the window, but not one thing could they see. They tried to open the kitchen door. It would not move.

"Are we bewitched?" cried Grandmother in amazement.

"Come upstairs!" cried Mr. Marshall.

Out into the cold hall they went and up the dim stairs. It was so cold that their teeth chattered. The upper hall was not quite so dark as the lower one. A strange, half light came through the window. Grandmother, Mr. Marshall, and the nurse peered out. They could not believe their eyes. They looked from one to the other with mouths open in surprise.

"Would you believe it possible?" gasped Grandmother.

"Never in all my life!" exclaimed the nurse.

"We are positively buried in snow!" cried Mr. Marshall.

They looked out on a strange world. Snow, snow was everywhere.

"Why, it is way up to the eaves of the barn!" cried Grandmother.

"It covers the doors and windows of the Jones' house," said Mr. Marshall. "You could walk right over and touch their chimney!"

But all the nurse could say was, "Never in all my life!"

The three watched for a minute and then realized that they were icy cold. They huried back to the warm kitchen.

4. Jessica, the Jersey

In the kitchen Nan was just opening her eyes. She had slept well. The nurse was proud of her. She would bring that baby through yet and have her as big and fat as any baby in town before she was through! That was the kind of nurse she was. Nurse bent tenderly over the basket in which Nan lay.

Suddenly the nurse straightened up.

"How am I going to get fresh milk for this baby?" she asked.

Grandmother and Mr. Marshall looked at each other helplessly. Then Mr. Marshall sat down heavily on a chair.

"Jessica the Jersey is in the barn," he said.

"But how is anyone going to get to her?" cried Grandmother.

It seemed to her too much to have such a tiny baby and such a sick baby and such a terrible storm all at once. Grandmother wanted to cry. But Nurse was not one to spend any time on crying.

"Get a shovel," said the nurse.

"What can you do?" cried Grandmother.

"Dig," was all the nurse said and she meant it.

Mr. Marshall jumped to his feet. Perhaps they could make a tunnel to the barn!

He hurried into his coat and pulled a cap down over his ears and tied a muffler around his neck. Nurse was ready before he was, with her coat and cap and gloves, and the second pair of rubber boots on her feet.

"Two can dig faster than one," said the nurse.

First came the problem of getting out of the house. On every outside door there was a double door put on for the winter to keep out the cold. The double door opened out. Mr. Marshall tried the kitchen door first. It was blocked by a wall of snow.

"You'll not get that door opened till the spring thaw," said the nurse.

It was no good trying to get out of a window. All had storm windows screwed tightly on the outside. But the side door was protected by a storm porch that Mr. Marshall put up every fall. Mr. Marshall and the nurse pulled open the door. They were faced by a wall of snow, but they had at least made a start.

"Well, let's start our tunnel," said Mr. Marshall.

Each took a turn digging while the other one carried the loose snow to dump at the end of the porch. For an hour they worked as hard as they could. Then they went back into the kitchen for a cup of coffee. They could hear Jessica mooing in the barn. Then Nan began to cry, a very small cry.

Nurse jumped up.

"Come on!" she said, and back she went to the tunnel.

Mr. Marshall followed with a lantern. Down into the dim, white tunnel he went, stooping low, for the passage was not high enough for him to stand straight.

At last the shovel banged against the barn door. Jessica gave a welcoming moo. She wanted to be milked.

She wanted to be fed and she was tired of all this cold, silent darkness. Mr. Marshall forced open the door. Into the darkness of the barn stepped the two diggers.

"Don't stop to milk her here," said the nurse. "I'm going to take her inside."

"What do you mean?" asked Mr. Marshall in dismay. "Inside what?"

"Inside the house," said the nurse. "I'm not going to run the risk of getting cut off from the milk supply again, not with that tiny, sick baby on my hands. No, sir!"

"But will Jessica come?" asked Mr. Marshall in surprise.

"Jessica will come if I say so!" said the nurse. She was a determined woman.

"Very well," said Mr. Marshall.

He led the mooing Jessica to the door. She peered into the white tunnel ahead. She put back her head. She wanted to be milked and to be fed, not to be taken out into a strange, wild world. Jessica braced her feet and refused to go farther.

"*Go on,*" said the nurse.

Jessica mooed all the louder.

"You pull and I'll push," said the nurse.

She got behind Jessica with the snow shovel. Now Jessica had no choice. She began to move slowly forward.

At Mr. Marshall's cry Grandmother opened the door.

"Goodness me!" cried Grandmother when she saw Jessica on the porch.

"Go right on in!" the nurse told the cow.

Jessica was not made to go around corners. She looked wildly to left and right. Then she bolted in through the door. Into the dining room she went and around the end of the table. *She had to.* The nurse was pushing her from behind with the snow shovel. Through the dining room and into the kitchen went Jessica. There Mr. Marshall tied her to the kitchen pump. Then he milked her.

"Now," said the nurse, "she can stay in the woodshed till we need more milk."

Grandmother was relieved. It did not seem quite the right thing to have a cow in the kitchen. Jessica was glad too. The woodshed was more to her taste.

In a few minutes Nan's milk was ready for her. Nurse was holding her in the big nursery rocker that had rocked all the babies in that house for over a hundred years. She pulled the chair close to the kitchen stove and she unwrapped only the tip of Nan's nose and her small mouth. Soon Nan was sucking as she should and Nurse was looking down at her with a satisfied expression on her face.

"We'll raise this baby yet," said Nurse, "blizzard or no blizzard."

It was three days before the village dug itself out of the snow. People tunneled from house to house to get food. People tunneled from houses to barns to feed cattle. Relief parties dug their way through the snow to carry food to people who were starving and medicine to people who were ill.

"There never was such a blizzard in the memory of men," said Grandmother, "and I certainly hope I don't live to see another!"

"And there never was such a cunning baby," said Mrs. Marshall as she looked down at Nan.

Nan was well and strong by now although she was

still very small. Nurse had gone back to her home at the foot of the hill. Jimmie and his puppy Bouncer were back from the Jones'. Bouncer was trying to climb into the basket beside Nan where there was no room for him.

"Down, Bouncer," said Mrs. Marshall.

Nan wrinkled up her tiny nose and doubled up her tiny fist. Mother and Jimmie both began to laugh at her.

Just then Father came in.

"Well, well, well," cried Father. "I certainly do enjoy having one boy Jimmie and one girl Nan. This is a *big improvement* for the Marshall family!"

But that was not the last "big improvement" that was to come to the Marshall household, as you shall see.

5. Pipes and Plumbers

Four years had passed since the great blizzard. People still talked of it and every time they told the story the snow became deeper and deeper.

"Soon it will be only the tops of the chimneys that were sticking out of the drifts," said Mr. Marshall, who could always see the amusing side of everything.

"It was bad enough as it was," said Mrs. Marshall, "without making it any worse!"

Jimmie was eight years old now and growing fast. He no longer wore curls and his sandy hair was clipped short. He was very brown from the summer sun and his nose was freckled. Wherever Jimmie went, Bouncer, the collie, went too. Bouncer was now as big as he would ever be.

In four years, Nan had grown from a tiny baby to a little girl with brown, curly hair and sturdy legs. She had a serious little mouth and a surprised expression in her brown eyes as though she found this world a strange and interesting place, as well she might. Any baby who had started this life during the blizzard of 1888 had reason to!

The old white house on Pleasant Street where the Marshalls lived had not changed at all in those four years. Indeed it had changed very little in the hundred years since Great-Grandfather Marshall had built it. The maple trees in front of the house had grown larger each year and the grass around it had grown greener. The old house had settled down comfortably on its solid stone foundations.

But changes were coming soon of which the old house knew nothing. Changes were coming of which Great-Grandfather Marshall had never dreamed. It was at the dinner table one fall day that Mr. Marshall announced the first one.

"I'm going to have running water put into this house," said Mr. Marshall.

Jimmie looked up in surprise and Nan stopped eating.

"Running water?" cried Mother. "Where, may I ask, are you going to get it from?"

"At town meeting this afternoon they voted to pipe water in from Green Lake," went on Father triumphantly. "The water main is coming down this street and a pipe will come right into this house. What do you think of that, my dear? It's time we had some improvements!"

"It certainly will be wonderful," said Mrs. Marshall, "if the workmen don't tear things up too much."

"Oh, no, no, my dear," Mr. Marshall assured her. "It will be nothing at all."

Mrs. Marshall did not feel as sure of that. Time would show.

"Think of the trouble and work it will save," went on Mr. Marshall. "No more pumping water and carrying it about the house in pails and pitchers."

"With baths and dishes and washing clothes, I've pumped enough water to float an ocean liner," said Mrs. Marshall and she gave a sigh at the thought of it.

"Now you'll just have to turn a faucet," continued Mr. Marshall, "and the water will run out. It certainly will be a big improvement."

Jimmie wanted to know how they could make a pipe long enough to bring water all the way from Green Lake to town and how deep the men would have to bury the pipe, and how the water could run up into the house. He asked so many questions that Mother said he must stop and eat his dinner while it was hot.

Nan at four did not understand at all what it was all about. She held her spoon halfway to her small mouth and asked, "How will the running water run?" She could not pronounce her r's as yet, so what she really said was, "How will the wunning water wun?" which made Jimmie laugh.

"The water will come running right into this house and when you want a drink all you will have to do will be to turn the faucet," explained Father, but Nan did not understand at all what he meant by that. Then she decided that at four one would do best to go on eating one's pudding and wait to see what this grown-up world was about.

At first there was no sign of running water that Nan could see. Workmen came and dug up the road and opened a long ugly trench across the lawn. Jimmie had to see everything that went on. He and Bouncer followed the men about and watched the pipes laid. They tracked so much dirt into the house that Mother was in despair.

"It will take all the running water in the world to get this kitchen floor clean," she moaned as she mopped it for the third time that day.

When the workmen had dug up the road and spoiled the lawn, they came right inside the house and began taking up floors. Nan kept close to Mother, but Jimmie was interested in everything that went on. Matters became worse and worse and one day the whole family had to go to the Jones' house for dinner. When they came home after dinner Father called them all to come to the kitchen.

"Now that's in, the worst part is over," said Father encouragingly.

Beside the kitchen stove stood a large shining copper boiler. Jimmy began to beat a tattoo on it, until Mother told him to stop. Then he ran upstairs to see what the men had done there since he last saw them.

"That's the boiler to heat the hot water," Father explained to Nan, but that meant little to her.

She stood looking at the light on the shining copper. But suddenly Nan was startled by a strange crash. Something was falling into the dining room. Nan ran towards the door.

Father and Mother were there ahead of her. The room was filled with dust. Plaster was flying through the air. It was hard to see anything.

"What is it?" cried Mother in dismay. "What has happened? Is the house falling down?"

But Father took one look. Then he ran quickly across the room through the shower of plaster and out into the front hall. Nan could hear him going up the stairs three steps at a time. The house shook.

"Hold on there!" shouted Father.

For answer more plaster fell on the dining-room table. "Keep perfectly still till I get there," cried Father.

When the dust and plaster had cleared a little, Nan could see something black sticking through the ceiling. Right through the ceiling it came and the hole around it was growing bigger and bigger as more strips of thin board and pieces of plaster fell. Then Nan realized that the black thing was one of Jimmie's legs. At the same second Mother realized what it was, too.

"Oh dear!" she cried. "Jimmie's falling through the ceiling!"

But Father had taken hold firmly of the rest of Jimmie. There was one last shower of plaster. Then the black leg disappeared.

When Nan and Mother reached the upstairs hall they found Jimmy and Father standing beside a large hole in the floor. Nan could see right through it and down into the dining room below. The plumbers had taken up the floor and left the place open. Jimmie had wanted to see where the pipes went to. He had stepped down into the hole by mistake. Right through the dining-room ceiling!

"He might have killed himself!" said Mother, who was looking a little white. She kept tight hold of Nan.

Nan peered into the hole. "Imagine finding the ceiling just on the other side of the floor like that!" thought Nan. There was a little dark space between and that was where the men were putting these mysterious pipes. Father was explaining it all to Jimmie, who did not seem to mind his tumble at all.

"He ought to understand these things," said Father. "It's good for him."

"But he oughtn't to step through the dining-room ceiling," said Mother, as she went downstairs to try to get a nap. "I shan't have a minute's peace till the work-men are safely out of this house!"

In another week the plumbers had finished in the Marshall house. One more week of confusion and then the floors were down where floors should be and the ceilings were up where ceilings should be. There were shining new faucets by the kitchen sink. Upstairs there was a new bathroom where the old hall bedroom over the kitchen used to be. Mrs. Marshall was glad to see the last of the workmen. She had had enough of them!

The next morning the running water was to be turned on.

6. The Old Tin Portable Tub

That night the children had their last baths in the old tin portable tub. The old tub had bathed them ever since they were born. Indeed it had bathed everybody who had ever had a bath in that house since Great-Grandfather Marshall's day. But tonight was the last night. Tomorrow there would be running water in the new built-in bathtub of painted white tin in the new bathroom upstairs.

It was a cool night in late autumn and mother rolled the tub into the downstairs bedroom and left the door open into the kitchen to let in warmth from the kitchen fire. She carried in a big kettle of boiling water from the stove.

"Stand back, children." That was what she always said every time she filled the tub. "Many a child has been badly burned with hot bath water."

Nan and Jimmie stood well back while Mother poured the steaming water into the tub. Then she added two pails of cold water and all was ready.

"In you go," said Mother as she popped Nan into the water.

Nan gurgled with pleasure as the water closed in around her small, plump person. Then she closed her eyes tight as Mother washed her face. When Mother washed, she did it in earnest. Nan gripped the side of the tub till the scrub was over. Then she squeezed the bath sponge full of water over herself.

"Out you come," said Mother as she lifted Nan in a warmed towel and gave her a rub.

Now it was Jimmie's turn.

"I'll wash myself," said Jimmie. So Mother went into the kitchen to see if the supper was cooking as it should.

"Be sure you wash thoroughly," she called back to him.

But Jimmie was not ready to settle down to business. He stuck one foot into the water and made some little ripples. Then he tried to pick up the washcloth with his toes. Suddenly with a whoop, Jimmie leapt into the tub.

But Jimmie had jumped in a little too fast. His foot slipped. He lost his balance. Wildly he gripped at the side of the tub. He sat down far too fast and too near the edge. There was a splash and two legs waved in the air. Jimmie tried madly to save himself, but it was too late—over went the tub. Water ran in every direction. The tub rose and fell and then came to rest directly on top of Jimmie.

Mother came running from the kitchen.

"James Arnold Marshall!" cried Mrs. Marshall. "Come out from under that tub!"

The tub wobbled uncertainly and then Jimmie's wet head appeared. He looked very subdued.

"I didn't mean to," choked Jimmie.

"Well, I certainly hope you didn't," said Mother, "but that doesn't make the floor any drier," and she ran for the mop.

Just then the front door opened and Father's voice sounded in the hall.

"What is the celebration about?" he called.

There was complete silence. Father came quickly through the kitchen into the bedroom. There was Jimmie peering out from under the tub. There was Mother with the mop, looking cross. It was Nan who could not help giggling.

"Jimmie tipped," she explained.

"Yes," said Mother, "and he made a great deal of trouble just when I was getting your supper."

Father burst out laughing.

"It's about time we had a built-in tub!" he cried.

"Everybody else has been able to bathe in that tub without tipping over," said Mother, but even she was beginning to smile.

Jimmie had scrambled out from under the tub and was scrubbing himself with a bath towel.

"We ought to celebrate the last bath in the old tin tub," Father declared.

"I think we have celebrated it enough," said Mother.

But Jimmie and Nan jumped for their slippers and bathrobes. Jimmie began to beat on the bottom of the tub.

"Come on," called Father. "We'll have a procession and escort the tub to the attic."

He turned the tub over and dumped Nan into it. Mother took one handle and Father the other. Jimmie snatched up two tin pot covers as they went through the kitchen, and clashed them together. Nan's eyes shone and she clapped her small hands together and kicked her heels against the bottom of the tub. Father began to sing and they all kept time.

Here comes the portable tub,
the portable tub,
the portable tub!
We've had the last scrub,
in the portable tub,
very last scrub,
portable tub!
We've had the last scrub,
We've had the last rub,

ERK

And Jimmie tipped over the
portable tub!

They climbed the two flights of stairs that led to the

attic and Father pushed open the door. Only a little
light from the last of the sunset came in through the
west windows. Old boxes and trunks and broken furniture stood under the eaves. There was Nan's crib that
she had outgrown and Jimmie's sled waiting for winter.
There was a strange musty, mysterious smell about the
attic that Nan liked.

In the dim light it was all the more mysterious, but
Nan had little time to look about. Father dumped her
out of the tub and caught her before she reached the
dusty floor. Then he swung her onto his shoulder and
began to sing as loudly as he could. Jimmie and Mother
pushed the tub under the eaves and then they all started
for the door.

Nan looked back at the old tin tub. "Good-by," she
called softly. "Good-by."

7. The Running Water

The next morning everyone in the Marshall house was up early. The running water was to be turned on! This was a very important day!

The plumber came at nine o'clock and he went down cellar with a very large monkey wrench in his hand.

"All ready now," he shouted.

The Marshall family stood in a row by the kitchen sink and waited for the water to be turned on.

"All right," shouted the plumber again. "Turn the faucet."

"You do it, dear," said Mrs. Marshall nervously.

Mr. Marshall put his hand cautiously toward the faucet. The whole family held its breath. He turned the handle. Silently they all waited. *Nothing happened.*

"Dear, dear," said Mother. "What's the matter?"

"Let me try," suggested Jimmie.

Just then the faucet gave a groan and a sputter and a strange, long drawn-out gurgle. Thump, thump, thump went the pipe. The Marshall family jumped back. The pipe was shaking violently now and seemed to have the hiccoughs.

"Is it going to burst?" asked Jimmie.

"Just wait a minute," shouted the plumber from the depths of the cellar. "There is air in the pipes. The water will come in a second or two."

So the Marshalls waited.

Suddenly there was a bigger gurgle than any that had come yet. One last hiccough and out splashed a stream of dirty, brown water. It came so fast and so hard that it splashed to the middle of the kitchen floor. The Marshalls moved back nervously towards the dining-room door. Up came the plumber from the cellar.

"Just let it run," he said, "and it will run clear in a minute."

The Marshalls were quite willing to "just let it run."

Soon the water became clearer as the rust from the pipe was washed away. The plumber stepped forward and turned the stream on and off to see if the faucet worked all right. Nan was amazed. One second there was a stream of water! The next second and there was none! It was like magic. Father and Mother and the plumber went upstairs to see about the new bathroom.

Nan and Jimmie stood by the sink and turned the water on and off for fun.

Jimmie tried putting his thumb over the hole in the faucet and holding back the stream of water. He could not quite cover the opening. A stream of water shot out sidewise.

"Look at that!" exclaimed Jimmie with pleasure.

But just then Jimmie lost control of the stream. He tried to turn the faucet off, but instead he turned the water on all the harder.

"Jiminy crickets!" he yelled.

The stream of water squirted towards Nan. In a second her hair was soaked and water was running down her nose. When Mother reached the kitchen, Jimmie was wiping Nan's face and there was water on the floor.

"I'll mop it up," said Jimmie quickly, as Mother looked about.

And so running water came to the Marshall house.

"Hot water and cold water and plenty of both," said Father proudly.

Washstands, pitchers and basins were carried to the attic along with the old tin tub. Everybody bathed in the bathroom now.

"But I'm going to have the pump left in," said Mother. "You never can tell just what might happen."

"Why, what could happen?" asked Father airily. "You might just as well be rid of it."

"No," said Mother firmly. "I'm going to keep the pump for a while longer. Big improvements may be big improvements but that's a very good well we have down under the house and it's served this family for many years.

8. The Running Water Does Not Run

It was something that happened that next winter which made Father decide to have the second big improvement.

Thanksgiving had come and Christmas had come and gone. Winter was well on its way when one very cold morning Jimmie and Nan woke up. They lay on their backs in their beds and wondered how soon they would have to step out into the cold. Jimmie could see his breath in the air and he pretended that he was smoking.

Suddenly they heard Mother's voice in the bedroom next door.

"*James dear,*" she was saying, "*something dreadful has happened! It is the coldest morning of the winter and the fire has gone out!*"

They could hear Father groan and turn over in bed.

"I can't imagine how it happened," went on Mother. "I put coal on the last thing, but the stove must have been too full."

There was another groan and then Father said as cheerfully as he could, "I'll be right down."

Next came the sounds of coal being shoveled from the stove and paper and kindlings being put in. Then a match was struck.

"My hands are so numb, I can hardly hold the light," said Father.

"It's dreadful," moaned Mother. "My teeth are chattering."

But soon came the sound of a cracking fire and the voices below became happier. Nan and Jimmie ventured forth into their icy-cold slippers and robes. Then they picked up their clothes and dashed for the warmth of the kitchen. Mother was just bringing in a pan of milk that had frozen stiff. She put it on the stove to thaw.

"Come close to the fire," she said to the children, "and hop into your clothes as fast as you can."

That was easier said than done in those days. Nan wore a shirt, and a corset-waist, and a flannel petticoat, and a white petticoat, and long stockings to pull up over long-legged underwear, and high buttoned shoes and a dress and apron that both fastened in the back. Every time that Nan dressed she had to fasten forty buttons. Jimmie had his troubles too.

"Oh, dear-me-suds!" he sighed as he struggled over the long black stockings that had to be pulled up over the long-legged underwear.

But at last the family was dressed and the milk thawed. Mrs. Marshall stepped to the sink to turn on the water.

"What's the matter?" she said in surprise. "No water comes out."

Father went quickly to the sink and tried one faucet then the other. No water! He looked worried.

"It was the worst night of the winter to have the fire go out," he said.

"What do you think has happened?" asked Mother anxiously.

"I don't think—*I know*," groaned Father. "The water in the pipes has frozen. When it thaws out, the pipes will probably burst!"

Nan looked up in amazement. Who would ever expect little black things like pipes to burst? Jimmie went over to the sink with renewed interest.

"Isn't there anything we can do?" he asked.

"No, we'll just have to wait and see what happens," sighed Father.

"Well, it's lucky we had the old pump left in," said Mother.

The room was very warm by now and little streams of water began to run down the window panes. The Marshalls sat down to a hot breakfast of oatmeal and scrambled eggs and bacon. Mr. Marshall was just beginning his second cup of coffee when a queer little sound came from the pipe by the kitchen sink.

"What's that?" asked Mrs. Marshall in surprise. "A mouse?"

There was no time for an answer. Suddenly water began to pour out of the pipe onto the floor. The ice in the pipe had melted and had burst open the pipe! Mr. Marshall leaped to his feet and rushed for the dishpan. Mrs. Marshall ran to the broom closet for pails. Jimmie reached for the mop, knocking down the dustpan with a crash. Bouncer began to bark and Nan climbed up in her chair to see everything that was going on.

"Light a candle for me, Jimmie," shouted Father, "and we'll go down cellar and get the water turned off."

Jimmie's hand shook so from excitement that he

burned his finger twice before he could light the candle. Then while Nan and her mother emptied buckets, Father and Jimmie started for the cellar door. Down into the clammy cold cellar they went. Nan could hear them moving about for a few minutes, then came Father's voice.

"Where is it that you turn off the water?" shouted Father.

"I thought the plumber showed *you!*" called back Mrs. Marshall. "I haven't the least idea!"

"I thought he showed *you*," groaned Father.

Up from the cellar came Jimmie and Father, and Jimmie went posthaste for the plumber. Luckily, the plumber lived only three doors away.

Mother helped Jimmie struggle into his coat and cap and mittens and sent him hurrying out into the crisp, cold air. Jimmie's face tingled as the wind blew against it. He ducked his head and ran as fast as he could.

When Jimmie and the plumber returned, Father was emptying buckets upstairs and Mother was emptying them downstairs. The plumber hurried down the cellar stairs as fast as he could run with his monkey wrench in his hand. There were sounds of hammering. Then the water began to flow more and more slowly through the pipes. At last it stopped altogether.

Mr. Marshall came downstairs wiping his forehead. Mother sank into a chair.

"Oh, these modern improvements!" sighed Mother. Just then there was a knock at the door. It was Mr. Jones. His pipes had burst too. Would the plumber come as fast as he could come? Up came the plumber from the cellar. He started for the Jones' house on the run with his monkey wrench in his hand.

Just as the plumber went through the door, he shouted back another bit of news.

"*Let the kitchen fire go out, or the hot water boiler will explode,*" called the plumber. "*It'll blow up the house!*"

Mrs. Marshall looked aghast. The boiler explode? Whoever heard of such a dreadful thing! How would they get on with no kitchen fire? Why had they ever started on these modern improvements anyway? Hastily she dumped the fire from the stove into the ash pan.

There was nothing to do but to light fires in the dining-room stove and the parlor stove. Luckily there was cold meat for dinner and Mrs. Marshall managed to cook some potatoes over the dining-room fire.

It was at dinner that noon that Mr. Marshall announced the next big improvement.

"This thing is not going to happen again!" he said firmly. "I am going to have a furnace put into this house."

"Oh, dear," sighed Mrs. Marshall. "Will they tear up the house again?"

"You can't have improvements without some trouble," said Mr. Marshall. Mrs. Marshall was quite sure of *that*.

Nan and Jimmie wanted to know more.

"The furnace will be big and black and it will be down in the cellar," explained Father. "Every room in the house will be warm."

Jimmie was delighted. He liked to have workmen around. Nan, who was more like her mother, was not so sure.

"It can't be done until next summer," said Father, "but I'm going to put in the order for it today!"

Father was as good as his word. Before night fell the order was in and the plumber had it written down in his book. A hot air furnace, pipes, flues, registers and everything needed to be put into the house of Mr. James Marshall on Pleasant Street before the first frost in the fall. Then Father ordered ten tons of furnace coal. After that he hurried home to see if there was room enough for all that in the cellar of the Marshall house, which had never been built for furnaces and big coalbins.

9. Kites and Chimneys

Jimmie and Nan watched the men carry the pieces of the new furnace into the cellar and put the great monster together. Nan thought that the furnace looked like a giant with long wriggly arms that reached up through the house. She wondered if it ever moved about and twisted at night. Jimmie said that was all nonsense. He wanted to understand how the thing worked and he asked the workmen a million questions.

There was a black register in the floor of each room for the heat to come through. Nan and Jimmie peered down to try to see where the openings went. One day Jimmie dropped a marble down the dining-room register. It clattered and banged so loudly that Mother came running out of the kitchen to see what was happening. Jimmie never found the marble again although he and Nan searched all the corners of the cellar for it.

The house was torn up even more than when the running water was being put in.

"It will be wonderful when it is done," Mother said to Mrs. Jones, "but it's simply too dreadful now! The dust and dirt and the plaster all over everything! You can't imagine what it's like!"

But Father was as interested as Jimmie. He was quite sure that everything was going to be wonderful in time.

"Remember the day that the pipes burst, my dear, and have patience," he told Mother.

"I'm perfectly sure I'll never forget that day," Mother assured him.

Nan was five now and Jimmie was nine. The summer had passed and the first chill days of the fall were coming on. The workmen were finishing up, and the new furnace was ready to use. The house was almost in order.

Father had taken Mother for a drive with a horse and buggy for the afternoon to give her a little rest and change which she certainly needed. Nan and Jimmie were at home alone. Jimmie had made a new kite and was trying to fly it. Nan held it for him and he ran across the lawn to get a start. For some time the kite refused to rise.

At last a puff of wind caught the kite. Jimmie gave a whoop and let out string. Nan looked happily up, up, up into the blue sky where the kite sailed above them. But then the wind changed and blew the kite toward the house. The big maple trees were in the way and Jimmie tried to pull the kite toward the open fields, but it would not be pulled. Right over the house it went. The string caught on the chimney, and the kite waved like a flag above it. Jerk as hard as he could, Jimmie could not get it down.

"Oh jiminy!" he muttered."

Nan looked on with sympathy. It was a shame to have Jimmie's kite caught up there and no way to get it down. Jimmie and Nan climbed to the attic to see if he could reach from the window and jerk the string loose. With some difficulty Jimmie raised the window. He leaned out so far that Nan trembled for fear he would fall, but still he could not reach the string. Nan ran down the two long flights of stairs for Father's hooked umbrella. Even that did not make Jimmie's reach long enough.

"It's no good," said Jimmie gloomily as he sat down on the old trunk in despair.

Nan sat down beside him, feeling gloomy too.

For a few minutes Jimmie sat and thought black thoughts. Then his eye lit on a trap door in the roof. There was a ladder on the wall leading to the trap door. The workmen used it when there were shingles that needed to be repaired or when something needed to be done to the chimney. Jimmie rose and wandered over to the ladder.

No one had ever told Jimmie *not* to go up the ladder nor to open the trap door, for no one had ever thought of his doing it.

"What are you going to do?" asked Nan uneasily.

"Just climb up a ways," Jimmie assured her.

When he reached the roof and the top-most rung of the ladder Jimmie decided to lift the trap door and look out. Perhaps he could reach the kite string from there.

Jimmie reached out as far as he could. The string was close, but just beyond his hand. He climbed out a little way. Nan could see first one black leg and then the other black leg disappear out the hole. Jimmie was gone from sight. She felt very small and very much alone.

As for Jimmie, he was balancing on the ridge pole and holding onto the chimney. He had never been on the roof before. He looked into the tops of the maples and down into an empty bird's nest that he had been trying to get all summer long. He could see over the roofs of the neighbors' houses as far as the village and the hills beyond. A cool breeze ruffled his hair and the kite flapped above him.

Jimmie reached for the string. It was hard to untangle. His coat was in the way. He slipped the coat off and threw it over the chimney so that it would not slip to the ground. Then he lay down and stretched his arm as far as he could. He gripped the string. A jerk or two, and the kite swung free. It floated off into the air as free as a bird, but it did not go too far, for the other end of the string was tied to the hitching post.

Jimmie wriggled back to the trap door and let himself down. Nan felt more comfortable when she saw him safe and sound. Of course Jimmie was Jimmie and nine years old and very clever. Still Nan was glad when the trap door was shut and Jimmie and she were on their way downstairs to untie the kite.

When Mother came home Nan wanted to tell her all about it, but something made her feel that it was best not to. Still she felt miserable and troubled and supper did not taste at all as it usually did. All at once Nan put her head down on the table and cried.

"Why, darling!" said Mother. "What is the matter?"

She felt Nan's head and then she looked serious. Father carried Nan upstairs and laid her gently on the bed. Then he went for the doctor.

When the doctor came he examined Nan all over and he took her temperature.

"Measles," said the doctor. "It's early in the season for them, but there are several cases in town."

So Nan lay in bed very hot and uncomfortable, and the kite and the trap door in the roof and the new furnace in the cellar were all forgotten for the time being.

But that night just before Nan tumbled into a troubled sleep she heard Jimmie downstairs saying, *"Where can my coat be?"*

"I haven't the least idea," said Mother. "You'll have to hunt for it yourself. You must learn to take care of your own things."

10.   Fire and Smoke

The next day Nan was all covered with speckles. Jimmie had to stay home from school. At first he was pleased, but when he found out that he couldn't play with the boys for over a week he looked at the matter in a different light.

"Why did you have to get the measles?" he said to Nan from the door of her bedroom.

"Now don't trouble Nan," said Mother firmly. "Go and look for your coat."

For that garment was still mysteriously missing.

"She thinks she's the only pebble on the beach," said Jimmie.

That was what all the boys were saying. Every year they find something else that they say on all occasions. You watch and you'll see. Nan wished she was a pebble on the beach. It sounded so cool and refreshing. Bed was very hot. Mother kept smoothing the sheets, but they got wrinkly again so soon. The room had to be darkened and Nan was very tired of having the measles. She did wish that something interesting would happen.

The day wore slowly on. At five in the afternoon, Father left his office. There was a crisp coolness in the air. He could smell the spicy odor of dried leaves burning. The maples were aglow with red and yellows. Barrels stood under the apple trees as he hurried past his neighbor's orchard. He must pick his own soon and put them down the cellar for the winter.

"It's a cool evening," thought Father. "With Nan ill, it would be a good time to light a fire in that new furnace. I'll slip down the cellar and start it as a surprise."

He let himself quietly into the house and went downstairs. Paper and kindlings soon blazed in the furnace. Mr. Marshall stood and watched them burn. There was a creak on the cellar stair. Jimmie peered down. Father put his finger to his lips.

"Come on down," he whispered. "I'm starting the furnace for a surprise."

Jimmie helped his father put in wood and then coal. The fire did not burn as well as Mr. Marshall wished it would. He looked at the drafts and did everything to them that he could think of doing.

"It's smoking," coughed Jimmie. His eyes began to smart.

"It's just because it's so new," answered Father. "Wait a minute."

Wait they did, but the smoke grew worse and worse.

"Jiminy!" whistled Jimmie. "It looks like a house afire!"

Mr. Marshal was troubled. He started upstairs to see what was happening in the rest of the house. He met Mrs. Marshall, looking very white and worried, at the top of the stairs.

"Goodness! What is happening?" she cried. "I'm so glad you've come. There's smoke pouring up every register in the house."

"It's all right," Father assured her. "I just started a fire in the new furnace."

But the smoke grew worse. The house was filled with it.

"Help me shut the registers and open the windows," cried Father as he raced through the rooms, sneezing and coughing as he went.

Jimmie and Mother and Father opened windows and closed registers, but more smoke came in than went out.

"What shall we do!" cried Mother in despair. "I can't have Nan start coughing!"

She ran into Nan's room.

"Measles or no measles, I've got to take you to the Joneses' and out of this smoke," said Mother.

She rolled Nan in a quilt and picked her up in her arms. Down the stairs through the smoke she went. What with the smoke in the air and the quilt over her head, Nan could not tell exactly what was happening, but this was better than just lying in bed. She did her best to peek out from under the quilt.

Out on the porch stepped Mrs. Marshall. The fresh cool air felt good to Nan after all that smoke. Suddenly Mrs. Marshall stopped.

"What's that?" she cried.

Through the quilt wrapped around her, Nan could hear a strange noise.

"Clang, clang, clang!" came the sound and the pounding of horses' hoofs on the road.

"CLANG, CLANG, CLANG!" It was nearer now. The horses' hoofs were swinging round the corner of Pleasant Street with heavy wheels rolling behind them.

Nan refused to miss anything as exciting as this. She pushed her head out from the quilt just in time to see the village fire engine draw up in front of the Marshall house.

"It's the fire engine!" gasped Mrs. Marshall. "Do they think the house is on fire?"

Mrs. Jones came rushing across the lawn. The firemen jumped down from the engine and began unwinding hose. The fire chief came running up the driveway.

"Where's the fire?" he shouted.

"Oh, don't, don't let them turn water all over my house!" wailed Mrs. Marshall. "I've just gotten it in order."

The fire chief looked surprised.

"Where's the fire?" he shouted again.

"In the furnace!" wailed Mrs. Marshall.

The fire chief stopped short and opened his eyes in amazement. "What do you mean?" he said.

"It's a new furnace and Mr. Marshall is down in the cellar and I'm so afraid something will happen to him and to Jimmie. But the house isn't on fire, I know it isn't!" cried Mrs. Marshall all in one breath.

The fire chief rushed into the house. In a few seconds back he came out with Mr. Marshall and Jimmie, all of them coughing, their eyes watering from the smoke.

"I can't see what's the matter with that furnace," said the fire chief, "the drafts are all right."

"But there's no smoke coming out the chimney," called one of the firemen who was waiting patiently with the hose ready to turn on the water. "The smoke's all coming out the windows."

"Oh, these new improvements!" moaned Mrs. Marshall.

Mr. Marshall and the fire chief ran down to the road where they could look up and see the chimney. Sure enough, no smoke was coming out of it.

"It looks as if there's something on it," suggested the fire chief. "I'll go up on the ladder."

The firemen brought a long ladder across the lawn. Jimmie followed right beside them. He wished he could climb it, but he knew it was useless to ask.

Mrs. Marshall sank into a porch chair and held Nan tight in her arms, but Nan's head was well out of the quilt and she could see all there was to see.

The firemen placed the long ladder against the side of the house and tested it carefully. Then the chief began slowly to climb up its length. Jimmie decided at once that he would be a fireman when he was older. With envy he watched the fire chief going up, up, up. Then suddenly something stirred in Jimmie's memory— something he had completely forgotten. His face grew red and hot, but no one noticed it in the dim light of the evening.

"Oh jiminy!" he muttered.

Jimmie walked over to the porch steps and sat down heavily. Mother looked at him anxiously. Was he getting the measles, too?

There was a shout from the fire chief.

"There's an old coat on top of the chimney," he cried.

"A coat!" exclaimed Mr. Marshall. "How could a coat have gotten up there?"

"Watch out and I'll throw it down," shouted the fire chief. "It's almost on fire.

Down to the lawn came a dark smoldering mass. Mrs. Marshall peered over the porch railing. Mr. Marshall gave it a kick with his foot.

"Why, it's Jimmie's coat!" cried Mrs. Marshall. "He's been hunting for it for two days."

Father could not believe his eyes and he looked blankly toward Jimmie. It seemed to Jimmie as if everyone in the world were looking at him. Father, Mother, the whole fire department, and all the neighbors as well. Jimmie wished that he could crawl into the new furnace and hide from view.

But he had to say something. Everyone was looking at him in amazement. He had to explain.

"I—I forgot I laid it down there!" he said. "I was getting my kite. The string caught on the chimney."

"You laid your coat on the chimney and forgot it!" gasped Mother. "James Arnold Marshall! You, *on the roof?* You might have been killed!"

The fire chief and the firemen did not take the matter so seriously. There was a roar of laughter. The firemen laughed and Father laughed and the neighbors laughed. Jimmie began to feel better.

"Now stop all this nonsense," said Mother, but she did not sound quite so serious either. "This child has the measles and I must get her back into bed."

Nan hated to leave all the fun and excitement. However, it was the fire chief who caught her up in his arms.

"Let me carry her for you, Mrs. Marshall," he cried. "I've had the measles."

He lifted Nan to his shoulder and put his helmet on her curly head.

"Here we go," he shouted, and Nan waved a good-by to everybody. Inside the house, smoke was no longer coming from the registers. The rooms were soon aired and then Mrs. Marshall closed the windows. Nan could just hear the sounds of the fire engine as it rolled down the street. She could hear Father and Jimmie coming into the house. They came up the stairs to her room.

"Is she all right?" asked Father.

"I hope so," said Mother softly. "She must go to sleep now."

Father walked over to the new register.

"The heat is coming up nicely now," he said. "The room will be warm and cozy in a few minutes. These furnaces certainly are a big improvement!"

"Yes," sighed Mother, "if—"

She looked toward Jimmie and Jimmie quickly decided to go downstairs to read the latest copy of his favorite magazine, the "Youth's Companion."

But before the winter was over even Mother admitted that the furnace was a success. All the stoves, except the kitchen stove, were taken down. Father had the old fireplace opened up and the family sat around the burning logs of an evening. Nan hated to leave it when bedtime came.

"Although," said Mrs. Marshall with satisfaction, "now that we have a furnace even the bedrooms are warm!"

11. Uncle Harry and the Aunts

Uncle Harry and the aunts were coming for Christmas! Everybody in the Marshall family was busy getting ready. Mother was stuffing the turkey. Nan, perched on a high stool, was polishing the extra teaspoons. Jimmie was supposed to be taking out the ashes from the fireplace and bringing up more wood. But a trail of ashes across the floor was all he had to show so far.

Nan had been six on her last birthday and she had started to school in September. Her dark hair hung in two braids on either side of her face and her brown eyes were open just as wide as ever.

Jimmie looked much the same as he had looked for some time. His eyes were blue, his hair sandy yellow, and his nose was covered with freckles. No one ever would have supposed from their looks that Nan and Jimmie were brother and sister.

There was a great surprise in store for Uncle Harry and the aunts this Christmas. The workmen had been at the Marshall house again. Father had had another big improvement put in. The Marshalls were the first people in all the town to have it. And that night, that very night, "IT" was to be turned on!

"Anyone want to drive to the station with me?" called Father.

There was a scurry for coats and mufflers and over-shoes, and Nan and Jimmy raced out the front door. By the mounting block stood a sleigh with two bay horses. Mr. Marshall took the reins from the driver and climbed in. Nan and Jimmie bundled in beside him and Father tucked the buffalo robe about them. It was a crisp cold day. The sun was about to set and it sent a soft rosy light across the snow.

Off the sleigh dashed toward the town, its bells tinkling. There were many sleighs hitched in front of the stores on Main Street, for people were out doing their last-minute Christmas shopping. Everyone seemed happy and gay. Nan wanted to sing for joy. She had a present for Father and Mother and one for Jimmie hidden safely at home.

Down at the station a few people were waiting on the platform, and the village hack was drawn up by the steps.

"Train is twenty minutes late," said the station master.

"Trains on this line are always twenty minutes late," laughed Father.

"If they aren't still later," grumbled the hackman, who had to meet all the trains.

"We have time to go for a drive," said Father.

Along the snowy road the horses trotted. The bells jingled and the sleigh slid so smoothly that it seemed to Nan they were flying. Jimmie wanted to drive, so Father let him take the reins. Down a steep hill they went. The boys who were coasting on the hill had to stand to one side in the deep snow to let the sleigh pass. Jimmie waved to his friends. On the trip back Mr. Marshall gave them all a ride up the hill and there were half a dozen sleds fastened to the back of the sleigh.

"Merry Christmas!" Nan shouted to the boys as they untied their sleds at the top of the hill.

"Merry Christmas!" they shouted back. Then off went the sleigh with a jingle of bells, and snow flying from the horses' heels. Back at the station there was still no train. Nan went into the stuffy, hot little waiting room to warm herself by the red stove. A dim lamp hung from the ceiling. Nan looked at it in amusement.

"Do you suppose 'IT' will be turned on when we get home?" she asked Jimmie. "It's getting dark."

Just then came the distant whistle of the train far down the track. Nan and Jimmie ran out onto the platform. Father had to stay with the horses. The train grew larger and noisier. Then with a rush and a roar the steaming monster came to a halt. Off jumped Mr. Robinson, who had been conductor on that train since before Nan was born. Soon Uncle Harry stepped out on the platform. His white mustache stuck out above the corners of his fur collar and made him look like a friendly walrus. Nan jumped up and down in the crowd and waved to him and shouted.

The aunts appeared right behind him. Mr. Robinson helped them down the steps. The aunts kissed Nan and cooed over her and said what a big girl she was getting to be. Jimmie helped Uncle Harry carry the bags around to the sleigh.

The sleigh was filled to overflowing, but at last everyone was tucked in with all the bags and the baggage as well. Mr. Marshall clucked to the horses and off they dashed toward home.

Nan kept looking ahead with impatience. It was dark by now and lamps shone from the windows of the houses along the way. At last they turned the corner by the Marshall house.

"Now watch out!" cried Nan to the aunts.

"Watch out for what, Nan?" asked one of the aunts mildly.

"Oh, oh!" cried Nan, for just at that minute the surprise happened.

The other houses along the street were lighted here and there by lamps that sent a soft light through the windows and out onto the snowy lawns. But suddenly as they watched, the Marshall house seemed to blaze up with lights, with so much light that the other houses seemed like pale, distant stars beside it. The parlor and dining-room windows gleamed brilliantly. The upstairs hall window and all the four windows in each of the bedrooms were aglow.

"Is the house on fire?" cried the littlest aunt in dismay. "James, James, what has happened?"

The aunts expected to see Father leap from the sleigh and rush down the street shouting "FIRE" at the top of his lungs. Instead he pulled the horses to a stop and sat looking at the house.

"That's what electricity can do," he said with great satisfaction. "That is what one would call a real improvement!"

Jimmie could hardly wait to jump out and run into the house, but the excitement of the moment kept him still. Nan took long breaths of the cold air and her eyes shone as though they too had little electric lights in them.

Then the front door opened in a flood of light and Mother's voice came across the snow.

"Aren't you people ever coming in?" she called gaily.

Father drove the team in at the gate and they all clambered out with much laughing and calling of "Merry Christmas."

Jimmie and Nan ran into the house and began turning the lights on and off. It was like magic. One second the room was as dark as a pocket. The next second you could see a pin in any corner. Nan looked at the little wires that ran across the ceiling and carried this new electricity.

"I thought they'd swell up when the electricity came into them," said Nan. "But they are just as little as ever.

"Oh, no," said Jimmie scornfully, "wires don't swell up."

He really knew as little about it as Nan, but he didn't like to admit it. But one thing Jimmie had found out. He pointed at the delicate glass bulb that hung at the end of the cord.

"If you drop one of those, or break it in any way, it goes off like Fourth of July," announced Jimmie.

Nan stroked the glass softly. It looked to her like a frozen soap bubble with fairy wires within, but Nan always had strange fancies about things. Jimmie just wanted to know how things worked.

12. "Listen, My Children"

After supper the neighbors began to drop in to see the new lights. Father took them down the cellar to show how easy it was now to see things there. Mother turned the lights on in the pantry and kitchen to show how every corner could be seen as clearly as in the middle of the day.

"My, it certainly is an improvement over lamps," cried the aunts, "and think of all the work it saves! No cleaning lamps, and cutting wicks and pouring kerosene! Think of the time it will save!"

"Perhaps yes and perhaps no," said Mrs. Marshall, who was not always sure about these modern arrangements.

She glanced at the row of lamps and candlesticks on the top shelf of the pantry. There was the dining-room lamp and the sitting-room lamp and the hall lamp and the bedroom lamps. She had filled them and cleaned them ever since she married Mr. Marshall fifteen years ago. Someone had filled lamps and cleaned lamps every day in that house back to the time when there was no kerosene, and people went to bed at night by candlelight. There had been a time when lamps were "big improvements."

Ned Jones had come with his mother to see the new

57

lights. Now Jimmie and he roamed about, turning the lights on and off. Mrs. Marshall watched them nervously.

"Now be careful, Jimmie," she warned. "Don't try any experiments. This electricity is a dangerous thing."

"That is just what I've been thinking," cried the littlest of the aunts. "Do you *really* think it's safe to have in the house, James?"

"Oh, perfectly, perfectly," said Mr. Marshall. "They have had electricity in the big towns for a long time now. It's only out here in the country that we're just catching up."

"Of course we won't keep all those lights burning all the time," said Mother to the aunts. "But just for tonight we'll celebrate. It's Christmas Eve."

Then Father shouted to the children to come and help him. He opened the door onto the back porch. A gust of cold, fresh air filled the kitchen. Nan peered out into the darkness. There stood a beautiful Christmas tree. It had come while they were away at the station and she had never known it!

The boys and Father soon had the tree pulled into the sitting room and set up by the bay window. Tall and beautiful it stood with its wide, dark branches ready to be decorated. Everyone helped and soon the tree was covered with tinsel and gay balls, and popcorn chains that Nan had strung, and colored candles ready to light.

Everyone laughed and chattered. When the tree was done they all trooped out into the kitchen for cookies and cake and hot chocolate. There was as much noise and laughter in the house as there was light.

Suddenly Father jumped to his feet. He had something to say to make them laugh and he beat on the table for quiet. Snatching up a frying-pan from the shelf over the stove, he waved it in the air and began:

"Listen, my children, and you shall hear—"

Father forgot the electric light just above him. He was used to watching out for lamps on tables. He was not used to watching for bulbs in the air! As he waved the frying-pan over his head, there was a deafening roar and a flash. Broken glass showered on the floor. The entire Marshall house was left in complete darkness.

No one moved for a second. Then Mother's terrified voice came through the blackness.

"Good heavens, James, are you killed?"

"I'm all right," said Father. His arm tingled from an electric shock, but he was all right otherwise. "But no one had better move. There's broken glass over everything, I'm afraid."

The kitchen was as dark as a cellar. Bouncer put back his head and gave a howl of despair. He was quite unnerved by what had happened.

But Jimmie and Ned Jones began to shake with laughter. They could not help themselves. Uncle Harry took it up. Even the aunts joined. Now that they had their breath again, after the suddenness of the shock, it all seemed very funny. Here they were in complete darkness while the "big improvement" hung useless above their heads!

"Are we going to sit here until morning?" Jimmie asked, when he could stop laughing.

"You stay where you are," Father ordered, "until I find the matches."

He trod on broken glass and he bumped into the furniture, but at last he found a box of matches by the kitchen stove. He lighted one and held it while Mother climbed on the chair and reached for a lamp from the top of the shelf of the cupboard. She was white and shaking, but she would not let anyone do it for her.

"There," said Mother as the soft light of the lamp made a circle on the kitchen table. "I shan't put these away quite yet."

Back they all went into the sitting room, laughing and talking all at once. Mother carried the lamp.

"Won't *any* of the light come on?" asked Nan in amazement.

"Father did something, I don't know just what," said Mother. "I don't think there'll be any more electricity in the house till the men come to fix it."

The room seemed very dim with only a lamp burning.

"Let's light the tree," suggested Nan.

No sooner said than done. In a few minutes the tree stood with all its candles twinkling. It lighted the room quite as well as electricity and was far prettier.

"And now," said Uncle Harry, "I think everybody ought to have one present apiece before we go to bed. Jimmie, open that package in the hall."

That night as Jimmie lay in bed, little giggles kept rising in his throat. It was too good to have Father be the one to put out the lights! Jimmie thought of the day when he had left his coat on top of the chimney. Now he and Father were even. All he would have to say was, "Listen, my children," the next time any of his plans went wrong. Jimmie wiggled his toes against the smooth sheet with delight. He had plans for a number of experiments with electricity that he wanted to try.

13.   The County Fair

Next to Christmas the county fair was the most important event in Jimmie's and Nan's year. The fair came in September. Jimmie and Nan looked forward to it all the summer. As soon as school was out in June they started planning what they would exhibit. For besides the horse-racing and merry-go-rounds and side shows and balloons, there were exhibits and prizes at the county fair.

Nan was finishing a patchwork quilt. She had sewed thousands of squares together, it seemed to her. She had made the smallest and neatest of stitches. Mother had helped her choose the prettiest pieces from the piece bag in the attic. And now the quilt had gone to Mrs. Howe to be made up. Nan was going to exhibit her quilt in the booth that was marked, NEEDLEWORK BY GIRLS UNDER TEN.

Nan felt very important. She did not think that there were many girls in town who had finished piecing a quilt before they were ten years old.

Jimmie had not pieced a quilt, but he had raised chickens. He sold the eggs to Mother, but he kept a careful record to show just how many eggs the hens had laid and what he had fed them. He had a crate of white hens with all the information about them ready for his part of the poultry show.

By six o'clock on the morning of the great day the Marshall house was astir. Mrs. Marshall was putting up a lunch to take along. Jimmie was feeding his hens and urging them into the crate. Nan was wrapping up the precious quilt. Only Father lay in bed and refused to get up till the usual time.

"Please get up!" begged Nan, and then she sat on his chest and jumped up and down gently until he was awake.

The exhibits had to be at the fair grounds by ten o'clock. Mother had ordered a horse and buggy from the livery stable to come at nine. Nan was ready long before that, and long before Father finally came downstairs for his coffee.

Mary had the coffee ready for him. Mary had come into the Marshall kitchen during the last winter. She had only just come to America from Ireland and she often told Nan and Jimmie stories of "the old country."

Jimmie was waiting by the mounting block to see which horse the livery stable had sent. He did hope it would be Lily, the little bay mare. He liked to drive her and he hated the slow old roan, Billy.

There came a sharp clatter of hoofs on the road and around the corner swung the buggy. Jimmy gave a smile of pleasure. Lily was slipping along at a brisk trot, her brown sides gleaming in the morning sun.

"Put the quilt in the back of the buggy and then tie the crate on behind," said Mother. "The lunch basket can go at our feet."

Mary brought out the lunch basket and the livery man

helped Jimmie carry the crate to the buggy and lift it into its place. Jimmy was to drive Mother and Nan to the fair grounds and then come back for Father at eleven. Jimmie liked to drive and was delighted to be the one to take charge of Lily.

Mother climbed carefully into the buggy, watching that her dress did not touch the wheel. Nan jumped in and settled herself carefully between Mother and Jimmie. The livery man untied the horse and Jimmie held the thick, leather reins tightly in both hands. The little tassel on the end of the long whip began to dance and flutter about as Lily started briskly off round the driveway, out the gate, and off toward the fair grounds. Father waved good-by and then went back to ask Mary for a second cup of coffee.

It was slow driving, for the road was crowded with wagons and carriages and herds of cows, and people on foot. A golden haze of dust rose from the road, and the air was becoming hot and sultry. Jimmie looked serious for once. He sat very straight and kept his eyes on Lily, who did not like being among a herd of cows or having her nose stuck almost in a crate of squawking hens. Jimmie talked to her and quieted her. Animals liked Jimmie.

It was half past nine when they drove under the big elm tree and into the fair grounds. Exhibits had to be in by ten. Ned Jones came running over to meet the Marshalls as they stopped. He helped Jimmie carry his crate of hens to the hall that housed the poultry show. Mother tied Lily to a hitching post and put a light blanket over her to keep off the flies. Then Mother and Nan went to the back of the buggy to take out the precious quilt.

Mother opened the back and then she called in a surprised voice, "Why, Nan, come here!"

Nan pressed close to her mother's side and looked into the back of the buggy.

"I thought you—" cried Nan, but her mother interrupted her.

"I thought you—" groaned Mother. It was too dreadful. There was nothing there. The quilt had been left at home!

"We'll have to find Jimmie and get him to bring it as fast as he can," said Mother hurriedly. "If we explain to the judges I'm sure they'll make an exception and let you put the exhibit in a little late. You worked so hard over it!"

Mother and Nan hastened to the hall where Jimmie had gone. They worked their way through the people and crates till they came to the boys' section. They searched till they found Jimmie's crate of hens all nicely labeled, but Jimmie was not there. At last they found Ned Jones.

"*Jimmie?*" he said in answer to their questions. "The last I saw of him, he went out the side door. Can I be of any help, Mrs. Marshall?"

"We must get Jimmie and have him bring out Nancy's quilt," explained Mrs. Marshall. "She forgot it and there's so little time to get it!"

"He must be outside," said Ned. "Come on and we'll find him."

They left the crowded hall as quickly as they could and went back to where they had tied Lily. There were many horses all standing patiently in a row, switching their tails to keep off the flies. But one buggy had already backed out of the row. It was moving rapidly toward the gate of the fair grounds.

"There goes Jimmie!" cried Nan in despair.

Jimmie was starting back to fetch Father. He was almost at the gate. Ned ran after the buggy, calling as loudly as he could. But the road was far less crowded now and Lily smelt home and oats. She wasted no time. Off she trotted as fast as she could go. Ned ran down the road shouting, but it was too late. A turn in the road and Jimmie passed the elm and was out of sight.

"I'm awfully sorry," Ned said, as he came slowly back. "Father's driven our team home and won't be back till Mother comes this afternoon."

Nan clutched Mother's hand. She winked back tears that insisted on rising in her eyes. She tried hard to remember that she was eight years old and had pieced a quilt even if it had been left at home by mistake. But for the moment she hated the music from the merry-go-round. She wanted to go away from the fair grounds and never, never, never come to a county fair again.

Mother went slowly into the hall and Nan followed. Then Mother began talking to some of the ladies who were arranging the exhibits of needlework.

"Dear, dear," said Mrs. Dana when she heard the news. "I'm so sorry."

"It's a shame," said another woman, "but if we let exhibits come in late, they'd be coming in all day."

"If it could be here by half past ten?" suggested a third who was watching Nan.

"Jimmie has taken our buggy back to town and I can't find anybody I know who has a horse and carriage here," wailed Mrs. Marshall. *"If I could only get a word to Jim-*

mie!" But Nan's heart sank. There seemed to be no hope. Suddenly an alert expression came over Mrs. Dana's face.

"I wonder if that new-fangled machine might be of some good after all," she cried.

"What do you mean?" asked Mrs. Marshall.

"You come with me," said Mrs. Dana. "My husband's been fussing with that thing for a week!"

14.   Talking Wires

Nan and her mother hurried after Mrs. Dana. They were too busy to notice the big black clouds were beginning to fill the sky. There was a grumbling and a rumbling to the west and the air was growing very hot. But they were far too excited to be troubled about that. They followed Mrs. Dana to a little house beside the grandstand.

"There's one of those new-fangled affairs in here that

you talk over," explained Mrs. Dana. "They have put it up and run a wire to the town hall to show people what the thing is. My husband has been down here for a week and I could hardly get him home for meals."

"Mr. Marshall has talked about that sort of thing," said Mrs. Marshall. "He saw one once in Chicago. They call them 'telephones.' Goodness! I never expected to use one."

"Well, sometimes it works and sometimes it doesn't and mostly it doesn't," laughed Mrs. Dana, "but it may help us now. If it gets us that quilt by half past ten it will be worth all the fuss the menfolk have been making over it."

Inside the house Mr. Dana stood by a strange box on the wall. There were two black tubes that stuck out from it. One was on the end of a string. There was a bell at the side and a little handle to ring it by.

"We want to catch Jimmie Marshall as he drives past the town hall," Mrs. Dana told him. "He left here about twenty minutes ago and he'll just be getting there. Tell him to get his sister's quilt and hurry."

Mr. Dana was becoming confused by all this talk.

"I'll try to get Jimmie," he said. First he rang the little bell at the side of the box. Nan watched eagerly. Then Mr. Dana took down one of the black tubes and held it to his ear. He spoke right into the other black tube.

"Hello!" shouted Mr. Dana so loudly that Nan jumped.

One could almost have heard him at the town hall, Nan thought, without any telephone between.

"Hello!" shouted Mr. Dana again.

Then he hung up the tube and rang the bell again.

At last Mr. Dana managed to get the box to say something to him. Nan could not hear what it was, but Mr. Dana began shouting, "Send someone out to get Jimmie Marshall as he drives past. Send someone out to catch Jimmie Marshall—Oh, all right, I'll wait."

Nan stood first on one foot, then on the other. It seemed as if that telephone were going to keep them waiting forever. She doubted if it had really said anything to a man way in town anyway. It seemed impossible.

"Looks as though we were going to have a storm," said Mr. Dana as they all stood and waited.

The rumbling of thunder was growing louder and seemed very near.

Suddenly Mr. Dana straightened up and held the black tube close to his good ear.

"Hello!" he shouted. "Oh, hello, is that Jimmie Marshall?"

Nan's eyes began to shine. Was the thing really working? Could they really talk with Jimmie when they were out on the fair grounds and he was in the town hall? She crept close to Mr. Dana— Yes, that was Jimmie's own voice, very faint and far away.

"Oh, Mother!" gasped Nan.

"Tell him to come right back as fast as he can," cried Mrs. Marshall excitedly. "And bring—"

"One thing at a time, one thing at a time," begged Mr. Dana. Then he shouted to Jimmie, "Your mother says to come back as fast as you can. Do you hear? Come back as fast as you can. Yes, that's it."

"He must be back by half past ten," cried Mrs. Marshall.

"Be here by half past ten," roared Mr. Dana.

"And bring Nan's quilt," cried Mrs. Marshall.

"What's that?" asked Mr. Dana.

"Tell him to go home and get his sister's quilt," cried Mrs. Marshall. "Quilt, Q-u-i-l-t."

Mr. Dana turned back to the telephone, "Go home and get your sis—"

But just then there came a roar louder than Mr. Dana's. There was a flash of lightning, then a crash. Mr. Dana dropped the black tube that he held in his hand and jumped nearly across the floor. Nan ran to her mother and hid her face in her mother's blue skirt. The crash of thunder was followed by a flood of rain. There were cries from outside as everyone on the fair grounds ran for shelter.

When Mr. Dana took up the black tube again, not a word could he get in answer from it. He rang his bell and he shouted until he was hoarse, but nothing happened. There was nothing to do but to settle down in the little house with the useless telephone and wait till the storm was over.

Mrs. Marshall tried to talk politely to Mr. and Mrs. Dana. She did not like the storm, she was worried about Jimmie, and she was very disappointed about the quilt. Now Jimmie was probably driving posthaste to the fair grounds through all this storm and with no quilt. These modern inventions did try her patience!

"In a few years there'll be one of these machines in every house in town," Mr. Dana was saying. "It is one of the most remarkable inventions of the century."

Mrs. Marshall was quite sure there wasn't going to be one in her house. Not if she could prevent it!

There was another crash of thunder and Mrs. Mar-

shall put her arm tightly around Nan. If she had her
way, someone would invent a machine to do away with
thunder showers. That would have some point to it!

Above the thunder and rain came the sound of the
big clock on the grandstand. Nan counted each stroke
with a sinking heart. Ten o'clock. Her quilt must be
there at the fair grounds by half past ten and as far as
she could see, there was no way short of magic to get
it there.

15. Jimmie's Drive

When Jimmie left the fair grounds, he drove quickly back to town. He noticed the clouds, but they did not trouble him. Jimmie did not mind thunder showers. He rather liked them. Lily stepped along briskly, her head up and her ears pointed forward. Jimmie held the reins loosely and let her go as fast as she wanted to go. The wheels of the buggy spun round so swiftly that you could not see the spokes. Now and again a stone flew back from Lily's heels.

Jimmie drove down the main street of town. It was almost empty. Stores were closed and everybody was down at the fair grounds. As Jimmie neared the town hall he saw a man standing by the roadside waving his arm.

"Whoa," called Jimmie to Lily as he tightened the reins and slowed her from a trot to a walk.

"Come inside," shouted the man. "They want to speak to you, down at the fair grounds."

Speak to him? At the fair grounds from inside the town hall? The fair grounds was three miles out of town! Then Jimmie remembered hearing about the new machine to be shown that year at the fair.

Jimmie stopped Lily. He jumped out of the buggy and followed the man into the basement of the town hall.

On the wall hung a strange looking box with two black tubes. The man picked up one of them and held it to his ear.

"Hello," he shouted.

Then he put the black tube into Jimmie's hand and pulled him toward the box.

"You listen there and you talk into that," he whispered excitedly.

Jimmie held the black thing against his ear and listened. At first there was only a murmuring and a rumble. Then a voice came.

"Hello," the tube said. "Is that you, Jimmie?"

"Yes," shouted Jimmie in amazement. "It's Jimmie Marshall."

How did the thing know his name right away like that?

There were dim sounds for a minute that Jimmie could not understand. Then the words came clearly again.

"Your mother says to come back as fast as you can, do you hear?"

"Yes," shouted Jimmie.

"Be back by half past ten," said the tube.

"It's nearly ten now," thought Jimmie.

Then the voice went on, "Go home and get—" Jimmie could not make out what he was to get.

"Go home and get your—" Suddenly there came a crash as the storm broke about them. It did not sound as loud to Jimmie as it did to Nan and her mother at the fair grounds. For the lightning had struck the elm tree just outside the gate and Jimmie was three miles away, but it was loud enough to make Jimmie jump.

When he took up the black tube again, not a sound could he get out of it.

"But I don't know what they want me to bring?" cried Jimmie. "And whatever it is, it's got to be out there in half an hour, and look at the rain!"

"You'd better go on home and see what they say there," suggested the man by the telephone.

With the rain running down the back of his neck, Jimmie ran across the sidewalk. He unhitched Lily, who was now soaking wet and miserable, and climbed into the buggy.

"Poor old Lily, there's no dry stable for you yet," said Jimmie.

Firmly but gently he turned Lily's head away from the livery stable and out toward the Marshall house.

Father was down at his office. There was no one at home but Mary, and she had been nearly frightened out of her wits by the storm. Jimmie made her sit down in a kitchen chair and listen to his story.. She could make nothing out of it. How could Mrs. Marshall send Jimmie word from the fair grounds to the town hall that she had forgotten something and then not tell him what she had forgotten?

But at last Jimmy made Mary understand. Something had been forgotten and they must hunt for it. Mary finally managed to give her attention to the matter at hand.

What could it be? Was it Mrs. Marshall's purse? Mary ran upstairs and looked in the top bureau drawer. Nothing was there. Was it the lunch basket? Mary peered out of the window to see if it had been left on the porch.

Nothing was to be seen from the window but a deluge of rain.

"Could it be that wee lamb's quilt?" asked Mary and she ran to the guest room where the quilt had been laid out open upon the bed.

There lay the quilt wrapped neatly in a sheet!

"That's it!" cried Jimmie triumphantly, "and it's got to be at the fair grounds by ten-thirty!"

"You can't go now with the rain and the lightning and the thunder," cried Mary. "Whatever shall we do?"

"Rubbish," said Jimmie.

He put on a rubber coat. "Mackintoshes" people called them and they were very new. Then he wrapped the quilt in Father's Mackintosh and carrying it carefully, hurried out into the storm.

Lily submitted with good grace and trotted along at a steady pace. Under the hood of the buggy Jimmie kept as dry as he could. The rain beat on him and it was hard at times to be sure that he was keeping Lily on the road. But there was no time to be lost. The rain was letting up now, and the black cloud was moving towards the east as quickly as it had come. They were almost at the gate of the fair grounds when Lily gave a sudden snort. She pricked up her ears and tossed her head. Jimmie leaned forward to see what was the matter. Then he pulled on the reins and brought Lily to a halt. There across the road lay the great elm tree. The lightning had struck it!

Jimmie looked the scene over. No getting through there! The road was blocked. He climbed out of the buggy and took Lily by the bridle. Gently he led her out into the field and around the tree. Lily looked wild-eyed and frightened, but into the fair grounds they went at last. Jimmie hitched Lily as quickly as he could and carried the quilt into the big hall. The clock on the grandstand was just striking the half hour. The storm was over. The people were coming cautiously out from cover.

When Mrs. Marshall saw Jimmie she could scarcely believe her eyes. She felt him all over to be sure that he was safe. Nan jumped up and down crying, "Did you bring the quilt? Did you bring the quilt?"

"Yes," Jimmie assured her. And then nothing would do but that she must race over to the hall to see it on the table labeled:

PATCHWORK QUILT—PIECED BY
NAN MARSHALL,
AGED EIGHT YEARS AND SIX MONTHS

"It's beautiful," said Mother.

Nan gave a sigh of happiness. She decided she liked county fairs after all.

Jimmie was wet, Lily was wet, and so were the fair grounds. Mother decided that they had all best go home and have a picnic lunch on the porch. Jimmie could come with Father for the horse-racing in the afternoon. Nan did not care. She was happy. Her quilt was safe, and where it ought to be.

"I'll telephone to tell you how the awards come out," said Mrs. Dana, "that is, if the men get the machine mended. Jimmie, you be down at the town hall at two this afternoon."

"Oh, thank you, Mrs. Dana," cried Nan as she gave her quilt a last loving look.

Men were beginning to clear away the old elm tree, but Jimmie had to lead Lily out into the field once again to get around it.

"I certainly am sorry to see that beautiful tree go,"

sighed Mrs. Marshall, "but I thought that lightning had gone right through me from the sound of it."

"You ought to have seen Mary," laughed Jimmie.

"Well, she found my quilt," said Nan with satisfaction. She was very fond of Mary.

16. One Long and Two Short

At a quarter past two Jimmie came whooping down the street on the run. He jumped the fence and vaulted over the porch railing. Father and Mother and Nan were finishing the picnic lunch and Lily was back at the stable munching her oats. Jimmie had dashed off at two o'clock to see if the telephone was mended.

"I got first prize," shouted Jimmie and he turned a handspring.

"And I," cried Nan, "did I get anything?" She could hardly wait for the answer.

"First prize! Both of us got blue ribbons," bellowed Jimmie. Bouncer, joining in, began to bark his head off.

Jimmie continued with his war dance, but Nan slid quietly into Father's lap and smiled up at him.

When the excitement had calmed a little, Father said, "But what about the telephone? I understand that saved the day. Oughtn't that to get a prize?"

Jimmie stopped his dance and sat down on the railing near Father.

"The boys say that they're going to put those machines into some of the stores and offices in town. I could hear as clearly over it as if Mrs. Dana had been in the next room. Couldn't we have one here?"

"It would be very convenient," said Father.

"Oh, James," sighed Mother.

"I could call up from the office when I was going to be late to dinner," suggested Father.

"It's better not to be late," Mother pointed out.

But Father and Jimmie won out and soon there was a talking box that hung on the wall of the kitchen. One long ring and two short was the Marshalls' call. Sometimes it worked and sometimes it didn't. Sometimes you got Mrs. Jones when you meant to get Mrs. Dana. It made Mary nervous.

"D-I-N-G-ding-dong," would go the telephone.

"Heavenly Biddy!" she would cry. "Couldn't you be still for a minute and me with an omelet in the pan!"

Mother laughed at Jimmie because he would call up Ned Jones when Ned lived next door. You could hear him answering the telephone at his end!

"You'll forget how to use your legs," said Mother.

One day Father came home to find Jimmie with the machine all in bits and laid on the dining-room table.

"I wondered why I couldn't get the house," exclaimed Father. "I've been trying for an hour! What are you doing?"

"I'll get it together again," Jimmie assured him. "I just *had* to see how it worked."

Father was as interested as Jimmie. Together they got it back on the wall, but the voices coming over it sounded strange and far away. When Mother ordered a beefsteak from the market, they sent up string beans instead! It took the repair man a whole morning to put the telephone to rights again.

"These big improvements!" said Mother.

"But what would you do without the running water

and the furnace and the electric lights?" asked Father.

"Oh well," said Mother, "they're different. They aren't new any more. They don't ring bells!"

Just then the telephone bell rang and she jumped up to answer it.

"There's no peace in this house," sighed Mother.

The telephone call was for Nan. Would she come over to have supper with her chum, Mildred Jones? Nan would and with pleasure. She would be there at five o'clock. Nan closed the kitchen door and ran out to ask her mother.

17. Bicycles

Bicycles, bicycles, bicycles! For some time everybody had been talking about bicycles. Jimmie Marshall wanted a bicycle more than anything in the world.

"Jiminy crickets!" he sighed as he watched two young men just home from college spin past on theirs.

The new bicycles were great improvements on the old ones. The old ones had a huge wheel in front and a small one behind. If anyone took a tumble from the high perch it was sure to be serious. But the new bicycles were different. They had two wheels the same size and were much lower. People all over the country were flying about on these new bicycles as though they could never bear to stay still again.

Jimmie cut the lawn every week all through the summer to earn money to buy a bicycle. It was hard work for Jimmie. When Nan had a task to do, she worked right at it until it was done. But Jimmie was always trying out new ways of doing things. First he tried to make Bouncer pull the lawn mower. Bouncer objected and finally went off after the Jones' cat, dragging the lawn mower behind him. Then Jimmie tried walking backwards to see how straight he could go. The lawn looked as though it had been cut with a pair of scissors.

"And old scissors at that," said his mother.

So Jimmie had to start in all over again.

"That boy would save himself so much time if he'd only do as he's told," sighed Mother.

"But he wouldn't have half as much fun," Father pointed out.

In September Jimmie helped Father pick the winter apples. When the last apple was picked Father paid him. Now Jimmie had enough money to pay for a bicycle. Jimmie and Father went down to order one that very afternoon.

But ordering a bicycle is not getting it. For three whole weeks Jimmie waited. It seemed to him that he would burst with impatience. Every day after school Jimmie came dashing home to see if the bicycle had come. Every day he spent the afternoon sitting on the mounting block with Bouncer, waiting. When would the bicycle come? Sometimes he sat and whistled all the afternoon and kicked his heels against the step, until Mother sent him on an errand to get rid of him.

"I'll be as glad as anyone when that bicycle comes," said Mother.

At last came the day when the expressman turned in at the gate with a large crate in his wagon. The crate was lifted into the kitchen with Bouncer running around it, barking as hard as he could.

Father had come home from the office early and he helped Jimmie. Out of its wrappings Jimmie lifted the new treasure. It was bright and shining. Never had Jimmie seen anything so beautiful in all his life. He wheeled it around the kitchen floor.

"Now," said Father. "Come outside and try to ride it!"

The whole family started to come too, but Jimmie

said that he preferred not to be watched. Nan peeked out of the window, but Mother sat down to her mending, and Mary went back to her work.

Father held the bicycle from behind while Jimmie mounted the seat. The bicycle wobbled uncertainly.

"Hold her straight, now!" cried Father and he started down the drive, pushing the bicycle.

The front wheel wiggled back and forth across the road. Jimmie clutched the handle bars and did his best to keep it straight. But suddenly there was a bounce and a bark. Bouncer leaped from the porch and dashed for Jimmie.

"Look out there! Down, Bouncer, down!" shouted father.

Bouncer was an old dog, but he was too excited to obey. A second later Jimmie and the bicycle and Bouncer all lay in a heap in the dirt. Bouncer tried to

lick Jimmie's face and Father shouted at him and pulled at the bicycle trying to rescue it.

At last dog, bicycle, and boy were untangled. Nan called Bouncer into the house and hooked the screen door so that he couldn't get out. Father wheeled the bicycle back to the mounting block and Jimmie started off again.

This time Jimmie steered very well. Father told him to try to push the pedals with his feet. But if Jimmie thought about his feet, he forgot about his hands. He watched his feet and paid no attention to where he was going. Into Mother's flower bed he went and over he tipped again. But the third try went better. Jimmie rode out onto the main road. Father gave him a good push, and this time off he rode all alone! He did fall off again near the Dana house, but that was nothing. Now he knew how it felt to pedal and to steer at the same time. It was only a matter of practice.

Jimmie settled down to business. By the end of the day he could ride quite well.

"Tomorrow I'll ride down and show the fellows," said Jimmie with satisfaction.

But, alas, something happened before tomorrow.

Jimmie was riding the bicycle to the barn to put it away for the night. Jessica, the new Jersey, was just returning from pasture. When she saw this strange new machine coming toward her, she put down her head and mooed in dismay. What was this? The man who was driving her shouted to her to go on, but go on she would not! Jimmie rang his bell. He tried to steer the bicycle to one side, but he too was startled by this un-expected meeting. Jessica swung to the right just as

Jimmie turned the wheel in that direction. Then over to the left went Jessica and over to the left swerved Jimmie. Crash! Over into the road went Jimmie. Jessica floundered about and then departed across the lawn, dragging the bicycle after her. The hired man ran after her shouting. Soon Jessica pulled her foot out of the wheel and galloped bravely off across the lawn leaving the bicycle behind.

Nan ran to Jimmie, who was getting slowly to his feet, with an expression of real misery on his face. This wasn't just a tumble like his earlier ones. The whole front wheel of the beautiful new bicycle was bent and twisted. It wobbled uncertainly as Jimmie limped to the porch with it. He was very sober. Nan blinked back tears.

Mother came running out to see what was the matter. She didn't care at all about the bicycle. All she wanted was to know that Jimmie was safe and to wash his bruises.

"They're nothing," muttered Jimmie as he and Nan sat down on the bottom step of the porch in despair.

It was Father who brought some comfort to Jimmie.

"It's only the front wheel," he said. "The repair man will have it mended in a few days."

"A few days!" groaned Jimmie. Father might as well have said months or years. A few days without his new bicycle seemed more than Jimmie could endure.

"How about a trip?" said Father thoughtfully. "I have to go to Boston tomorrow. I could manage to take you and Mother if you'd like it. It won't hurt you to miss a few days of school."

Boston? Jimmie had never been to as large a city as Boston. Railway trains, street cars, elevators, all sorts of

interesting things flashed through Jimmie's mind. The
new bicycle would be mended and waiting for him
when he came back! The world became bright again
for Jimmie.

Grandmother was to come to stay with Nan, and Mildred was coming to spend the night with her. Nan was to
go on the next trip, if she was a good girl while they
were away.

"As if Nan was ever anything else but a good girl,"
laughed Father. "I'd like her to be very naughty just
once."

"Now don't put ideas into that child's head," said
Mother as she hurried Father off to pack his bag.

At eight the next morning the old station hack drove
in at the gate. Mother and Father and Jimmie climbed
into the musty darkness. Nan stood at the gate and waved
good-by. Off they went and broken bicycles were forgotten for a while.

18. The Homecoming

The trip to the city was a great success. Jimmie spent all of one morning riding up and down in the elevator in the hotel. He had never seen one before and was interested in how it worked. The elevator man taught him how to run it. Jimmie and Father rode on every electric car that Jimmie could discover. Electric cars were just coming in. They were a big improvement over horse cars. Jimmie and Father sailed down the harbor. They went to the circus. They went to the old North Church where Paul Revere hung his lanterns.

But the most interesting part of all was the new machine that Father bought to take home with them. Jimmie and Father spent a morning in the shop looking at it and talking with the man who sold it to them. It was a machine that talked and played music from records. "Phonographs," they were called.

"As if there wasn't enough talking around without having a machine to do it too!" said Mother. "First you have to have a telephone so you can talk all over town and now you have a machine that talks to you. My mother used to say that silence was golden. As far as I can see there's going to be very little silence in the future."

The trip home was a great event for Jimmie, too. He

always liked to ride on the train and he knew a great deal about things like engines and freight cars and brakes and couplings. But never had Jimmie ridden in the locomotive. Father knew Mr. Robinson, the conductor on the train, very well. He had known him for years, ever since Nan was a baby. Soon Father and Mr. Robinson were deep in talk. Jimmie sat on the arm of Father's seat and waited.

At last there was a pause in the conversation and Jimmie saw his chance.

"We have to wait twenty minutes at the junction," said Jimmie. "Do you suppose that I could climb into the locomotive, Mr. Robinson?"

Mr. Robinson took out his watch and looked at it and considered.

"We ought to be at the junction in fifteen minutes, but we're twenty minutes late," observed Mr. Robinson.

"Trains are always twenty minutes late on this line," laughed Father.

Mr. Robinson considered further. Jimmie wiggled on his perch and nearly fell into the aisle as the train went around a curve. Mr. Robinson snapped the case of his watch shut and put it away.

"Weather's dry for this time of year," was all Mr. Robinson would say.

But Jimmie was not discouraged and when they reached the junction, he stayed close beside Mr. Robinson. Mr. Robinson helped the passengers off the train. Then, suddenly, he turned to Jimmie.

"Come along," he said. "Joe White is in the cab."

Down the length of the train they went, Jimmie close behind Mr. Robinson. They passed the passenger coaches and the smoking car and the baggage car and then they came to the steaming, puffing engine. Happily Jimmie sniffed the wonderful smell of steam and oil.

Joe White was leaning over a valve with his oil can in his hand. Mr. Robinson called up to him and explained what Jimmie wanted. Jimmie gazed up at him with longing. Oh, how he wanted to climb up that ladder and into that cab! Mr. White hesitated for a moment. Then he nodded his head. In another minute Jimmie was beside him.

When the train was ready to start Mrs. Marshall jumped up to look for Jimmie.

"Where is he?" she cried. "He may be left behind!"

"He's quite all right," Father assured her.

The train gave a jerk as it started. Father persuaded Mother to sit down and look out of the window. But every few minutes she moved uneasily.

"Where can Jimmie be?" she asked anxiously. "Is he in the smoking car or the baggage coach?"

At last Father broke the news to her gently.

"He's probably running the engine," said Father.

"James!" gasped Mother, "and he has on his best suit! He'll probably wreck the train or fall out the window!"

"He's fourteen and he's got to learn to look after himself," laughed Father.

It was a nervous trip for Mother. At each station she longed to go to see if Jimmie were safe, but Father would not let her.

"Let the boy take care of himself," said Father.

"He's never in his life been able to take care of anything, let alone himself," groaned Mother.

At last the Marshall family reached their own station.

Mother and Father stood on the platform surrounded by their bags. They watched Jimmie climb down from the cab of the engine. He had a black streak of grease across his nose. His hands were black with coal dust. But he was grinning from ear to ear. He looked so happy that even Mother did not have the heart to mention what had happened to his best suit.

"Thank you, Mr. White," called Jimmie.

From the window of the cab Joe White smiled back at him.

"That boy's got a head for machines," he shouted cheerily to Mr. Marshall.

Mother and Father and Jimmie carried the bags to the station hack which stood by the platform. The hackman jumped down to help them in.

Mother sank back on the cushion.

"I do wonder where Nan is," she said. "I thought she would be down to meet us." Suddenly Father leaned forward and nearly fell out the window.

"My goodness, what do you think of that!" he cried.

Father opened the door at the other side of the hack and jumped to the road as the old horses started off at a slow and sober gait.

"What's the matter with Father?" cried Mother. "It's just someone on a bicycle!"

"Jiminy crickets!" yelled Jimmie. "That's my bicycle!"

Perched on the bicycle, her two braids sailing out behind her, was Nan. The bicycle was far too big for her. She could reach the pedals only part of the way round. But she gripped the handle bars tightly and did her best.

"Stop the hack!" cried Mother, "and let me get out before that child is killed!"

The hackman pulled up his horses. Mother opened the door to get out, but Nan jumped lightly off the bicycle and wheeled it to the side of the carriage. Father stood beside her wiping his forehead with his handkerchief.

"Hello!" she called gaily.

"Nan!" gasped Mother. "What have you been doing!"

"Well, the bicycle came home all mended," explained Nan, "and I just began to ride it a little at a time and it was very easy once you started."

"You might have smashed it again!" said Jimmie ruefully.

"But I didn't," said Nan.

"You might have been badly hurt!" said Mother.

"But I'm not," cried Nan. "I've been riding all over town."

"Everybody will think she's a tomboy," sighed Mother.

"And a good thing if they do!" laughed Father. Now that the shock was over he was quite pleased with Nan. Girls as well as boys ought to do interesting things.

"Now let's see you mount it and start off," he said to Nan.

Nan had to push the bicycle to the side of the station platform to climb up. But in a twinkling she was on it and pedaling away. Father stepped into the hack and the hackman started up the old horses. They followed Nan slowly down the street.

"I'll never dare go away again," sighed Mother.

Three weeks later the express man again drove in at the Marshalls' gate.

"Another crate!" exclaimed Mrs. Marshall. "It must be that new part for the furnace."

But what the crate held had nothing to do with the furnace. Out of the wrappings Father lifted a new bicycle. It was smaller than Jimmie's and it was for a girl.

For a minute Nan could say nothing. She opened and shut her mouth, but no words came out. Her eyes shone brightly and it almost seemed as if she were going to cry.

"What about it?" asked Father. "Do you think you could use this?"

"Do you think I could use it?" cried Nan and then she threw her arms round her father's neck.

Soon Nan and Jimmie were flying all over town on their bicycles. The next summer Father bought one, too. He tried to persuade Mother to learn to ride. But Mother preferred to sit on the porch.

Father and Nan and Jimmie rode all over the countryside. They had picnics and they went swimming in a nearby lake. Father said that the exercise made him feel ten years younger.

"But it's lucky it doesn't make Nan feel ten years younger than she is," said Father, "for then she wouldn't be born yet."

Nan said it made her feel ten years older than she really was and at her age that was quite as good.

19. Mr. Marshall Returns

It's funny that Father doesn't say what train he's coming on," said Mrs. Marshall as she folded a letter that had just come from Mr. Marshall.

"I'd like to meet him at the station," said Nan. "He's been away a whole month and he wasn't even here for my birthday."

Roller skates and a box of candy had come from Chicago. Nan had liked them very much, but she did miss Father. He often went on business trips, but never before had he stayed away a whole month.

He was coming back today, but he had not told them on what train. Long before the time for the first train Jimmie came rushing into the house, jumping up the steps in one leap and slamming the front door behind him so that the old house shook.

"Jiminy crickets!" shouted Jimmie. "Come on out, everybody!"

Again there was a resounding slam from the front door. Mother put her hand to her head.

"What has gotten into that boy?" she said.

But she hurried downstairs as fast as she could and Nan ran after her. The front porch and the front lawn looked quite the same as usual. Everything was neat and in order, and the first crocuses were poking up through the green grass. Mother and Nan looked about, thoroughly mystified. What did Jimmie mean?

Mother and Nan went cautiously down the front walk to the gate. They saw Jimmie come running up the road and waving his arms about as if he were mad.

Then Mother and Nan saw what he was waving at. Down the road came one of those new-fangled "horseless carriages" that people were talking about. It was moving slowly along and it made a chugging sound. It was the first "horseless carriage" that Nan or her mother had ever seen, although they had read about them in the papers and seen pictures of them. "Automobiles," people called them.

This one was really coming towards them and moving smoothly along. Then—

Mrs. Marshall gave a gasp. "Your father is driving it!" she cried.

Mr. Marshall sat very erect on the front seat. He was watching the road carefully and giving all his attention to what he had to do. A crowd of boys was running along behind the car. "Get a horse!" they shouted. Nan could hardly believe her eyes, but just then the "horseless carriage" turned neatly in at the Marshall gate and came to a stop beside them.

"Well, how do you like it?" said Mr. Marshall to his astonished family.

"Well, I never in all my life!" was all Mother could say.

Jimmie and Nan showered him with questions. Yes, the automobile would really go. Hadn't they just seen it? It did belong to them, and, if Mother were willing, they could go for a ride sometime. Not now! Father wanted some breakfast.

When Father was seated at the table with coffee and eggs before him, Mother said nervously, "James, do you think it is safe?"

"I've been running one around Chicago for nearly a month," said Father. "Of course you have to be careful and not go more than twenty miles an hour."

"Twenty miles an hour!" cried Mother. "That is perfectly dreadful!"

But Jimmie and Nan thought it would be fun.

Late that afternoon, after he had hurried down to his office, Father said that he would take Nan and Jimmie for their first ride, if Mother were willing. Mother wasn't at all willing, but she knew she had better keep that to herself if there was to be any peace in the family.

It was five o'clock when Nan and Jimmie climbed into the waiting car. Father had to take a crank and go to the front of the automobile to start the engine. He whirled and whirled the crank until all of a sudden, the car began to shake and to quiver as if it had a chill.

Nan looked nervously about her. Father hurried around and wiggled some mysterious things by the steering wheel. The engine kept on going, but the car did not shake so much and Nan felt a little better about it.

"Now don't go far and don't be late," warned Mother anxiously. "I won't have a peaceful moment till you are all safe back home."

"Don't you worry," they called.

"I certainly shall!" she answered as they drove through the gate.

Father shifted several levers and made some changes

with a thing he called "the gears" and then they sped along smoothly through the town. It seemed very strange to Nan not to have a horse in front of them. It seemed to her as if she were going to tumble right out over the dashboard into the road.

Jimmie was watching everything that Father did.

"Will you teach me to drive it?" he asked.

"Sometime soon," said Father, "but you'd better wait a little. These things are still pretty new. They'll be more reliable as time goes on."

This one was reliable enough to suit Jimmie and Nan. Mile after mile it carried them through the soft, spring evening. It seemed to Nan as though it ate up the road ahead, so swiftly did it speed along.

"And now," said Father, "we must turn and start for home or Mother will be worried."

They were spinning along the road toward home and supper when Father muttered something to himself.

There in the road ahead was an old gray farm horse pulling his wagon home after a hard day's work.

"I don't suppose horses will like these new automobiles any better than they did the trolley cars when they were new," said Jimmie.

"They certainly don't!" said Mr. Marshall.

He stopped his car and waited by the side of the road. But the old farm horse had no intention of going past this strange monster. He began to rise slowly into the air on his hind legs.

"Get up, Jehoshaphat!" shouted the farmer behind him.

It did no good. The farmer jumped from the wagon and ran to the horse's head. He tried to calm Jehoshaphat and to lead him gently toward his barn, but Jehoshaphat would have nothing of that. He plunged about like a great rocking horse. Finally the farmer succeeded in turning him down a quiet lane and tying him to a post. Then he came back to have a look at this new machine.

"I've heard of those," the farmer said to Mr. Marshall, "but this is the first one I've seen. How do you like it?"

"They're the greatest invention of the age," said Mr. Marshall. "You'll all be running around in them in a few years."

The farmer laughed at that idea and said there'd probably be a good many people killed first.

It was time to be getting home and Mr. Marshall climbed out of the car to start the engine. He took out his crank and gave several vigorous turns to it. *The engine would not start.* Mr. Marshall looked worried and then he cranked and cranked some more. The new automobile stood silent and still by the roadside.

Mr. Marshall opened up the front part of the car. He called to Jimmie to bring him a screw driver. He tightened several little screws while Jimmie watched anxiously. Then he cranked some more. Nothing happened.

It was growing very dark. Jimmie went with the farmer to the house farther down the road to get a lantern.

20. The Old and the New

Mrs. Marshall was growing very worried. She kept going to look out of the window. No sign of the new automobile! She kept stopping her work to listen. No sound of a chugging machine coming down the road.

"I do wish they'd come," she said to Mary, who had come to the door to ask what to do about supper.

"You'll just have to keep things warm," Mrs. Marshall told her. "I'm afraid that these new inventions are going to make meals very irregular."

Mrs. Marshall went to the telephone to ask friends if they had any news of her family. Each house she called had the same answer. Mr. Marshall had been seen speeding down the road to the west of the town. No one had seen him come back.

At eight o'clock Mary came to the door again. Supper would be spoiled. Wouldn't Mrs. Marshall take a bite herself just to keep her courage up? Mrs. Marshall drank a cup of tea, but that was all she could swallow.

"If I only knew where they were," she said. "I would get a buggy and drive out that way. But I might just miss them. They may all be brought in dead any minute!"

At nine o'clock Mrs. Marshall went next door to talk with Mr. Jones. He came out to the porch with her and together they walked up and down the sidewalk. Mrs. Jones stood on the porch wishing she could help.

"The night is black as a pocket," said Mr. Jones. "There are a dozen roads going in that direction."

"Oh dear!" said Mrs. Marshall.

At ten o'clock there came the sound of a horse's hoofs on the silent road.

"Here comes someone," called Mr. Jones. "It may be word from your husband."

They all hastened down the road—Mary and Mrs. Marshall, the Jones family, and several other neighbors who had joined them.

Jog, jog, jog, came the old, white farm horse. He seemed very tired and he moved very slowly. He was pulling something which did not look like a buggy or a farm wagon.

"James!" cried Mrs. Marshall.

The old white horse was pulling Mr. Marshall's new automobile. Inside it sat Mr. Marshall and Jimmie. Nan was asleep between them.

In another minute Nan was in her mother's arms and everybody was talking and laughing as hard as they could.

"These new inventions—" roared Mr. Jones, holding his sides.

"They're wonderful when they work—" laughed Mrs. Jones.

"Heavenly Biddy!" laughed Mary, "to think of them starting out so fine and coming back behind an old white horse!"

The next day Mr. Marshall found out what the trouble had been. He had run out of gasoline. Soon he had the car running all over the town and was inviting all his friends to ride. By afternoon he had even persuaded Mother to go. But first he had to promise not to run faster than ten miles an hour!

21. Knickers and Old Shirts

What would this family say to a camping trip for a vacation?" suggested Father one day at dinner.

Jimmie was sixteen now and Nan was twelve and the year was 1900. In the year 1900 there were no Boy Scouts or Girl Scouts, and camping was quite a new idea to the Marshall family.

"We'll drive to the shore of a beautiful lake that I know of," went on Father. "There's a tiny log cabin way back in the woods. You can reach it only by water. We'll hire two boats at a farm at the other end of the lake and paddle down to the cabin. We'll take everything we need for two weeks and we'll live like savages in the wilds."

Nan and Jimmie were very pleased at the idea. Mother was not quite sure about it, but where her family went she went too, so that was that.

At last the day came when the automobile was loaded and the family ready to start. Mr. Marshall had a new car. It was larger and better than the one that he had brought back from Chicago. Indeed other people in town had bought cars since that day when Mr. Marshall had driven home the first one.

Mr. and Mrs. Marshall sat in front in the new car. Nan and Jimmie perched on top of the blanket rolls and food boxes. Grandmother had come to stay with Mary, and the two of them stood on the porch waving goodby.

Father honked his horn and away they started.

By afternoon they reached a farm house at the edge of a lovely lake. Father had written ahead for boats and two were waiting by the landing—a rowboat and a light canoe. A tall farmer in blue overalls and a big straw haying hat came out of the house to help them load the boats. Father drove the car into the barn and left it beside a surprised cow who was waiting to be milked.

Jimmie and Nan looked longingly at the canoe.
"Could we, Mother?" asked Nan.

Jimmie was a very good swimmer, but he was care-less. Nan was careful, but she could not swim far. Mother considered, but Father said yes.

"That is," went on Father, "if Jimmie will remember where he is and not try any experiments."

Jimmie promised. He and Nan climbed carefully into

the graceful little boat. Jimmie pushed off and they moved smoothly and gently across the lake.

Nan gave a little sigh of happiness. It was all so beautiful! There was no house in sight except the farmhouse they were fast leaving behind them. Thick woods came down to the water's edge. There were tall pine groves with soft, red brown pine needles beneath the trees.

Suddenly Jimmie jerked his paddle. Nan gripped the sides of the boat. What was Jimmie up to now?

"Look to your right," he whispered excitedly.

Nan turned carefully. Two slender deer were drinking from the lake. As the boat neared they leaped lightly into the underbrush.

The boats rounded a wooded point of land and there was the little log cabin set back among the trees. Nan could hardly wait to explore it. Shutters were closed across the windows and the rough wooden door. It looks as if it is asleep, Nan thought.

As Father opened the door of the cabin, there was a scuttle of field mice and a chattering of squirrels. Father shooed them out and opened the shutters to let in the warm soft air. There was nothing in the cabin but a few rude benches and tables. It did not take long, however, to bring it to life. Canvas cots were put up and gay blankets were spread out. Cans and jars of food were arranged on the shelf. Three cooking pans and a coffee pot were hung on nails. Nan picked a bunch of wild roses and put them in one of the tin cups.

Father and Jimmie brought loads of firewood and soon a campfire was burning on the rocks in front of the cabin. Nan helped Mother cook supper over it. The sun was setting as they ate on the rocks. The entire family

were so tired and so sleepy, that they could stay awake
no longer. As a new moon rose over the lake, they
tumbled into their beds.

Only the little woodland animals were awake. They
chattered and scolded at these newcomers. They sniffed
at blankets and shoes and they ate everything that they
could find that was meant to be eaten and some things
that were not meant to be eaten, too. In the morning the soap was gone, and Mother's cold cream jar was
empty.

Father was the first one in the lake the next day. Nan
and Jimmie were not far behind him, but nothing would
persuade Mother to go in.

"It's time for breakfast," she soon called.

Big bowls of corn mush cooked over the open fire
tasted better than anything that Nan or Jimmie had ever
eaten before. The family sat on logs near the fire. The
sky was clear and blue. The lake lapped gently at the
rocks beside them. When Father had finished eating, he
stretched himself out on a rock in the sun.

"This is my idea of a vacation," said Father.

Nan washed the breakfast dishes at the edge of the
lake and fed the minnows with the scrapings from the
mush kettle. Jimmie stood watching her. He had the
coffee pot in his hand.

"Let's see if we can catch some," said Jimmie and he
reached for the minnows.

The tiny fish flashed away from his hand.

"Oh, Jimmie!" cried Mother in dismay.

In reaching for the minnows, Jimmie had absent-
mindedly laid the coffee pot down on the water. It was
floating out toward the middle of the lake.

"My coffee pot of all things!" wailed Mother.

Father sat up and Jimmie started towards a boat. But as they watched, the coffee pot filled with water and sank.

"Oh, dear me!" said Mother.

"We'll get it," Father assured her. "We'll have a diving match. The one who gets the coffee pot won't have to chop any wood for two days."

Father and Jimmie rowed the boat to the spot where the coffee pot had sunk. There it was nestled against a rock at the bottom of the lake. They took turns diving for the lost treasure. First Father held the boat in place while Jimmie dove. Then Jimmie took the oars and Father tried.

At Jimmie's third try there came a whoop of triumph. He waved the coffee pot in one hand.

"Well, I'm glad to get that back," said Mother.

There was much to be done in camp. There were

three swims each day. There was fishing and there were
long paddles on the lake and walks in the woods. There
were sings by the campfire at night and reading aloud.
Each day the Marshall family grew sturdier and
browner.

Nan gave up gingham dresses and wore an old pair
of Jimmie's knickers. Father wore a favorite old suit
that made him look like a tramp. Even Mother hemmed
up a long skirt so that it was well off the ground and
wore an old shirtwaist turned in at the neck. Jimmie
refused to wear anything but a bathing suit.

"We're a perfectly respectable family," sighed Mother, "but anyone seeing us would take us for gypsies!"

22. The Trip Home

The two weeks were over. The boats were packed and the Marshall family were going home.

"Oh dear!" sighed Nan. "The little house will have to shut its eyes and close its door and go into another long sleep till we come again!"

It seemed strange to see Father dressed in a neatly pressed suit again, and wearing a stiff white collar. Mother held up a long, dark skirt as she walked over the rocks to the canoe. She had on a fresh, starched white shirtwaist with a high tight collar. High on her hair was perched a hat held in place by two long hat pins. Jimmie wriggled uncomfortably in his blue serge suit with the long trousers. Nan had gone back to blue gingham and had on shoes and stockings for the first time in two weeks.

The blanket rolls were in the rowboat and Nan climbed on top of those. Jimmie invited Mother to ride with him in the canoe.

"You'll have to be careful," warned Father. "Mother doesn't like the water."

For no one had been able to tempt Mother into the water or onto the water since they came.

At first Mother had sat up very straight and stiff in the canoe and gripped the sides firmly with both hands.

110

But as Jimmie paddled along smoothly, Mother lay back against the pillows. Jimmie watched her with a smile.

At last Mother gave a little sigh and said, "It really is quite lovely out on the water. I've enjoyed this trip more than I ever supposed I would."

Father heard her and he gave a laugh.

"Wait till you reach home and then see what you'll say," he called.

Mother sat up straight again.

"James!" she cried. "What has been happening at home?"

Not a word would Father answer.

Grandmother and Mary came running out on the porch to meet them.

"Well," cried Grandmother, "you certainly are a brown and healthy-looking family!"

"It was so nice!" cried Nan. "You can't imagine how nice camping is until you've done it. We cooked over the open wood fire."

"Yes," joined in Jimmie, "we wore old clothes and we swam in the lake instead of taking baths in an old bathtub!"

"You can't think how peaceful it was," said Father, "with no telephone bell ringing for two whole weeks! No automobiles dashing past the house day and night!"

"We carried our drinking water from the sweetest little spring in the ferns back in the woods," added Nan. "We went to bed by fire light."

"Well, well," said Grandmother, when she had a chance to say a word, "carrying water and cooking over wood and going to bed by fire light! It sounds to me the way we used to live *before* we had these modern improvements. We used to think it was a hardship!"

"You must come next time," cried Nan.

"No, my dear!" said Grandmother firmly. "No camping for me! I'm old-fashioned enough to like modern improvements! But speaking of improvements, aren't you coming to see the new kitchen?"

"New kitchen?" cried Mother weakly. "James, what have you done?"

Out to the kitchen the family trooped. The walls were pale green instead of the old brown and the woodwork was shining white. A new white sink stood by the window. The old coal stove was gone. In its place stood a smaller one with little handles to turn.

"A gas stove!" exclaimed Mother. "That is an improvement!"

Mother looked very pleased, and Nan jumped up and down with pleasure.

"I never saw a prettier kitchen!" cried Nan.

She wanted to try to cook on the stove at once. But Mary had supper ready for them, and the Marshalls were all very ready themselves for all the supper that Mary had to put on the table.

Before Nan went to bed that night, she took one last look at the new kitchen. As she stood at the door she realized that something had gone. Something that had been in the kitchen ever since she could remember. The old black pump no longer stood by the kitchen sink. For a second she was sorry and then she thought, "It must be dull for it standing there all day and never being used. It's just as well." Still she did miss it!

Mother was calling and Nan ran upstairs to bed.

Conclusion

It was one summer day several years later that Jimmie lay on his back in the hammock on the front porch. Nan and Mother were sewing beside him and Father was reading his newspaper.

Suddenly there came a sound far, far up in the sky. Father laid down his paper and stood up to see what it was. The strange buzzing came closer.

"Is it a swarm of bees?" asked Mother.

The Marshalls looked at each other in surprise. Then Jimmie gave a whoop and jumped over the porch railing at one jump. He raced to the middle of the lawn and stood looking up with his head thrown far back.

Father, Mother and Nan joined him by way of the porch steps. There against the blue of the sky, was a tiny black speck. As they watched, it grew larger and larger and the buzzing louder and louder.

"It's an aeroplane!" gasped Jimmie.

The first plane that the Marshalls had ever seen passed over their heads and disappeared far beyond the tree-tops.

"That is perfectly amazing!" said Mr. Marshall.

"My!" gasped Jimmie more to himself than to anyone else. "I'd like to be up with that fellow!"

"James Arnold Marshall!" Mother said with all the firmness that was in her. "Once and for all times let me say that that is one thing I would *never* consent to!"

But Mary was calling them for lunch and the Marshalls turned back to the house. Jimmie's feet were on the ground, but his fancy was far away. Little did Mother dream of what was to come in the years ahead!